TERRA
BLANCA
INSURRECTION

ZOË
ROUTH

Copyright Zoë Routh, 2023
Cover art – Damonza
Author photograph – Paul Chapman – modeimagery.com
Typesetting, book design – Damonza
Published by Inner Compass Australia Pty Ltd.
For more information about the author
Zoë Routh
Email: zoe@zoerouth.com
www.zoerouth.com

ISBN-10: 978-0-6455212-5-2 Ebook
ISBN-13: 978-0-6455212-6-9 Amazon Paperback
ISBN-13: 978-0-6455212-8-3 Paperback

READ THIS BOOK FOR FREE WITH
THE BOOKISH E-JOURNAL:

https://www.zoerouth.com/bookish

For my Outward Bound friends:

Thanks for a lifetime of laughter, adventure, and love

PART ONE

CHAPTER ONE

Insurrection hadn't been on the menu.

Governor Rylie Addison spent the day in happy oblivion, preparing a sumptuous feast. Creamy blue cheese and parsnip soup, slow-cooked ribs with a thick, rich glaze, golden roasted nugget potatoes, and a mountain of fresh salad. Dessert was a dark chocolate brownie with raspberry coulis. None of the provisions were available on Terra Blanca. She'd raided the stores of confiscated contraband. Regan would not approve. But he was on night security detail tonight. Thank goodness. The man was a bore.

There was a knock as Rylie sliced truffles into tiny wafers for the beans. She wiped her hands on a tea towel and hurried to the door.

"Come in! Great to see you, Luke."

Luke Finnegan sauntered into the room and surveyed the spread approvingly. He stroked his immaculate goatee.

"Glad to see some greens," he said.

"Of course! I knew you'd appreciate that. What do you say all the time? They have a 'calming' effect?"

"Vegetables take us back to the Earth." Luke sampled a bean with appreciative grunts. "We need to be grounded. Especially on a floating, man-made island."

"Even if these are grown hydroponically?"

"Are these from the greenhouse or are they contraband?"

"These particular beans are from the contraband Regan and his crew seized two days ago. But Jerome tells me our beans will be ready for the first harvest in a week."

"That should help stop the grumbles."

"I hope so. No one is happy about supply rations since the storm."

"It's not just the rations, Rylie. You know that."

Rylie kept her head down as she laid out the cheeses. She didn't want to go over the issue of the storm survivors again. She'd enacted executive override powers to ensure the additional three hundred people were allowed to stay. What was she supposed to do? Their homes were gone, they had nothing – they were going to starve. Still, the council was divided on the issue. She hoped this dinner would help build a few bridges. Except for Regan. He was never going to come around. He was still angry that the newcomers had bumped his family back from settlement by at least another twelve months. More likely two years. She clenched her jaw at the memory of the heated discussions. But she knew she was right.

There was a knock and the door swung open as Kate Watkins stepped into the room.

"Hello there! How are you? Is that *cheese*? Oh my God! Rylie, you've outdone yourself this time," Kate said as she scooped a big, oozy chunk of brie into her mouth.

She was an impetuous woman who crammed her voluptuous body into clothes a size too small and wriggled in testy discomfort at council meetings.

"How is the waste management system going?" Luke asked Kate as he poured her a glass of cabernet sauvignon. He looked at the label. Australian. Margaret River. His favourite.

"We're lucky we're not drowning in shit right now," Kate said. She licked her fingers clean of brie before cutting a piece of blue cheese for a seeded cracker. "The team has been working all hours to make sure the tanks can handle the extra load. And those bloody people!" She huffed as she took a bite of the cracker. She chewed with noises of delight then swallowed. "Those damn ingrates. We've been running around getting the water going to their accommodation. Making sure the toilet system doesn't back up. And they're constantly on us to fix this and fix that. To get them a missing ladle or pan."

"Wasn't Eve going to handle the storm survivor requests?"

"No. Jerome's doing it. Thought it would sit better seeing as he's in charge of food supply and all. Besides, Eve is too busy writing articles about their complaints. That daughter of yours is a real bleeding heart, Rylie."

Rylie brought the bread board to the table and set it down carefully. She steeled herself against the criticism of her daughter.

"Someone needs to advocate for them," Rylie said.

Rylie hacked at the sourdough, then put the knife down and breathed deeply to control her reaction. The yeasty aroma filled her senses and she sighed. Good food was such delight. Would it be enough to temper frayed spirits?

"There's a difference between advocating for refugees and berating the people who are trying to help them," Kate said as she popped a few grapes into her mouth. "Where is she, anyway? I thought she was joining us."

"I'm here."

Rylie's daughter Eve stood at her bedroom door with hands on hips. She was a tall, lanky beauty with a regal nose and heavy-lidded brown eyes. Even at seventeen, she was becoming more and more like her father, thought Rylie.

"The storm refugees deserve to be heard. And the criticism of work is totally justified." Eve walked over to the table and crossed her arms with a scowl at Kate.

"You ought to go along and help the sewerage team. Find out for yourself if they are really deserving of your criticism," Luke said.

"I don't need to shovel shit in a tank to know that leaving an overflowing toilet for two days is not good."

"Nonsense. We cleaned that up."

"What about the pile of linen you used to mop it up? Your team left the shit-stained sheets stinking up a room."

"That was an oversight. They were busy getting the plumbing working so we could actually wash the sheets. There was a lot going on that week," Kate said with a flick of her hair.

"Charming dinner conversation," Rylie said. "Maybe we could let it go for tonight? This dinner is meant to be a celebration. A reward for hard work."

"Some are working harder than others at the moment," Eve quipped.

"Come on, Eve," Luke said. "Grinding that axe is not

going to get the results you want any faster." He waved a chunk of sourdough at her, scraped it through a bowl of hummus, popped it in his mouth and winked. Eve rolled her eyes. Luke chased the bread with a sip of water. "Where is Imo?"

Imogen Bussle was Rylie's deputy and Head of Innovation. She was a pint-sized hellion. Quick-witted and passionate, Imogen drove Terra Blanca industry with the energy of a wild cowboy charging across the plains.

"She should be here soon." Rylie finished slicing the bread, filled the butter dish, and placed freshly picked flowers in her favourite vase at the centre of the table. "Why don't you have a seat, and we can have the first course." She bent her head to savour the sweet scent of the lilies of the valley.

"Is Jerome coming?" Luke asked.

"He had other commitments," Rylie said.

Kate snorted and chuckled to herself. "Is that what we call it these days? That man just can't keep it in his pants."

"And Regan?"

"He's on night shift security detail."

"So, we're having a council dinner, a celebration dinner, without two of the council members?" Luke's eyebrows wrinkled upwards.

"It's not an official council dinner," Rylie said. She felt the heat rise in her cheeks. She sensed Luke studying her as she ladled the parsnip soup into a bowl for each of them.

"You didn't tell Regan, did you?" Luke brushed his hands of crumbs and tilted his head to consider Rylie more thoroughly.

"No," she sighed. "No, I didn't."

"He doesn't know this is where the contraband ended up, does he?"

"No. He doesn't." Rylie rested the ladle on the drip saucer and lifted her head and her flaming cheeks to take in Luke's hardened gaze.

"That might not have been so wise," he said quietly.

"Maybe not. But it's done now. Besides, I checked it with Vincent. His analysis showed that this would be the most judicious way to dispose of the contraband. And it seemed like a better alternative than letting the community fight over it and turning the whole thing into a witch hunt."

"A.I.s don't always get it right. They often lack the broader context."

Rylie could feel her shoulders tighten.

"The food should have gone to the survivors," muttered Eve.

"And watch the original Terra Blancans protest again?" Rylie could feel frustration push the words from her mouth, regretting it almost instantly as the torrent of emotion took over. "Terra Blancans have been on half rations since the storm. Giving the refugees this food would only have fanned the flames. The food needed to be eaten or it would have been wasted. And I thought you all deserved some appreciation for the work you've been doing to get the second floating pod up to speed for the new arrivals. So here we are." She gestured to the sumptuous spread before them.

"Except for Regan. And Jerome," said Luke.

"And Imo. She's not here yet," interjected Kate as Rylie opened her mouth for a rebuke. "Have we figured out who the smugglers are?" Kate drained her glass of wine and reached for a refill.

Rylie took a moment to compose herself as Luke sat and served himself some of the beans. "Not yet. Regan has a few suspicions, but so far, no definitive leads." Her voice was flat, her balloon of emotion deflated.

"Who does Regan think it is?" Eve asked.

"He didn't say."

The door swung open and Imogen bustled in.

"Hiya!" Her face was flushed as if she'd been hurrying. "Got caught up with the Dopplebots. A funny malfunction just then. They couldn't receive any signals. We had to do a comms reboot. Readings on the robots were down everywhere."

"That's strange. Is it fixed now?" Luke asked.

"Not yet. They're investigating. Looks like some kind of jamming tech or satellite glitch. The weird thing is there was an unexplained power surge just before they went dark, like an unscheduled transmission, but we can't tell what was sent or where it went because the logs were wiped by the blackout. Wow, this is some spread! Some damn smuggler will be pretty pissed he missed his shipment. Whoa, Rylie – why so glum? This looks amazing."

Imogen slid into a chair and picked up her spoon. She leaned over the bowl and sniffed. "Blue cheese? Oh, my word! That would have been hard to find. No one is running cattle anywhere near the mainland these days. Probably brought up from the US Midwest. They're still managing to hold out with some live herds. God knows how in this climate. Speaking of which – where is Mr Hardcore Climate man? Off apprehending someone for using too much biofuel?" She slipped a spoonful of soup into her mouth and closed her eyes in delight.

"He's on security patrol," Luke said. "He wasn't invited."

Imogen put her spoon down. "He wasn't invited? Does he know we're eating the contraband?"

"No, he doesn't. I'll tell him later, all right?" Rylie said. Her voice rasped with irritation. "Eve, I made your favourite – ribs," Rylie said. "Remember when we had these? It must have been close to our last meal in the old town."

"I remember," Eve said, clipping her words.

Her daughter's dark eyes flashed. Rylie tried not to recoil, then simply sat down. She stared at her bowl then lifted the spoon and began a slow and deliberate consumption of the exquisite soup.

The five of them ate in silence. After a while they started sharing polite comments about how tasty it was. Rylie said nothing and cleared the bowls. She hated herself for her petty anger, but she was at the edge of her tolerance. She was only trying to do the right thing. Damned for doing something nice, derided for making the tough calls that needed to be made. She was sick and tired of the criticism. She threw the spoons in the sink.

The clatter pulled her up short. Time to regroup.

She returned to the table with a steaming plate of ribs that made her mouth water. It had been years since she'd had real meat. It was the same for all of them. Secretly she thanked the smugglers for stuffing up their run and falling foul of Regan's relentless vigilance. She would never admit this to anyone, of course. They'd have to torture her first.

She offered the plate of ribs for Luke to help himself. He chose a small serve and placed it gently on his plate.

Imo, Kate and Eve followed with no comments as Rylie's ire continued to burn the air between them.

Rylie made a concerted effort to shift her emotional tone. "Kate, how are things going with the second platform? How far are we away from having all the residences connected to water and power?"

"Power's on. Drinking and cooking water is on. Effluent and waste management is problematic, but we're getting on top of it."

Eve huffed and made a face. Rylie ignored her.

"How are things at the Wellness Centre, Luke?" She continued her check of the team.

"All clear. Still three patients with head injuries amongst the mainland storm survivors that I'm holding for observation, given there is no furniture in the second residential platform. Any word on that? When can we let them bring their belongings on-site?"

"That's really up to Kate and her crew. The engineers need to sign off on water and power before we load the platform any more than it is now with the extra bodies."

"Not long, not long now," Kate said as she drilled her teeth with a toothpick. The gristle niggled her.

"Imo, I hear there might be some people with programming and IT skills among the survivors. Have you had a chance to check the report?"

"I had a quick look but it's really Jerome who needs the help. We've doubled demand with these storm survivors. With the rations, and the broken machinery from the storm, food production is struggling again. I told Jerome he could recruit first and then I'd check in once we stabilise food production."

"That's great. We need some good news. The protests haven't been pretty and people seem quite upset at the moment," Luke said.

Imogen offered Luke the cheese platter, which he waved away.

"Come on, live a little, Luke. You're not going to burst into flames if you eat something a little naughty. Besides, we can't let this go to waste. People would have our heads if they knew we were letting good chow like this go uneaten." Imogen elbowed him and put the platter down so she could load up a few crackers with the remnants of the cheese. Then she poured herself a generous glass of wine. "Cab sav – yummo. Nice and dry, just the way I like it." She smacked her lips as the wine slipped down her throat.

"Any more before dessert?" Rylie returned to being the perfect host.

The plates were messy with rib juice, the cheese was all but gone, and her guests leaned back and sighed in sat-isfaction. Maybe this wouldn't be such a difficult evening, after all.

Then there was a pounding on the door and everything went to hell.

Regan led the charge. The door slammed open and he pushed his hard, muscular body through the doorway. His bulk filled the room and his voice boomed.

"Governor Rylie Addison, you and the council are under citizens' arrest for gross abuse of power." Regan's ice-blue eyes blazed and his lips pressed together in grim determination. Four other young men crowded in behind him, wielding pipes and tools from the greenhouse, like a medieval mob. Even through the haze of shock, Rylie recognised them. After six months, she knew all the faces but not the names of the three hundred Terra Blancan residents. These boys were Regan's crew from maritime patrol.

"Regan, what is the meaning of this?" Imogen demanded. She leaped to her feet and brandished a fork.

"Sit down, Imogen," Regan said. Something in the flint of his voice and the tilt of his towering frame cut down her resistance. Imogen stared at him, then lowered herself to perch on the chair, still clutching the fork.

Regan held her gaze and let the silence suffocate. Rylie watched as he stared at each one of them in turn. Kate's face was pale and her sausage fingers batted her chest. Imogen glared, knuckles white from gripping the fork. Luke leaned back in his chair, arms crossed. He considered Regan and his fresh-faced mobsters with a detached curiosity. Eve was staring intently at Rylie. She mouthed "Do something!" with a furious look. The accusation hit Rylie in the chest. Eve was always complaining about Rylie's indecisiveness. Her tendency to placate rather than challenge.

Rylie opened her mouth to say something but found no voice. Regan threw her a warning glance.

"As I was saying, gross abuse of power. Even the kid is in on it." He eyeballed Eve. "Quite the little smuggler, aren't we? Caught red-handed trying to dispose of the evidence." He waved at the remains of their dinner. The platter of ribs, thick and greasy, creamy rich cheeses with figs and grapes, a few bottles of wine. Rylie's stomach churned. Out of the corner of her eye, she saw Eve's frightened face.

"Eve?" Rylie asked. "But that's ridiculous! She's just a child, she's not a smuggler! Eve, tell him!"

But Eve's face betrayed the truth.

"Yes, tell him, Eve!" Regan mocked. "Turns out your holier-than-thou daughter's got a pretty nice side hustle going on, with her 'to hell with Terra Blanca' attitude. And I don't need to tell you that the risk to biosecurity is huge. Her selfish actions have put the entire Terra Blanca food production enterprise in jeopardy."

"Now hang on, Regan!" Rylie managed to croak. She felt the shock at her daughter's subterfuge conflict with the need to defend her against Regan's accusations.

"I don't want to hear it, Rylie. I'm sick of your two-faced hypocrisy. You're very happy to toe the line, except when it comes to looking after yourself and your own. I see you've been living it up while the rest of us labour and starve." Regan's face was mottled red. "Well, the jig is up, Governor, and it's time for a reckoning. Boys, take these 'supplies' to council chambers as evidence."

Regan bent to peer into Rylie's face. His breath was sour with onions and coffee. Rylie could feel the heat of his body rolling off him.

"You and the council will stay right here until we're ready for the trial. Be a good girl and behave, won't you?"

The trial? The threat seared her mouth shut in shock and she just glared at him.

"Don't do anything stupid, Governor. We'll be posting a guard right outside." Regan's goons grabbed the plates of food and bottles of wine, jostling the startled council members aside roughly. One of them elbowed Luke with malicious intent.

"No need for that," said Luke. "We can all still be civilised, can't we?" Luke shuffled his chair to the side to allow the young man better access to the cheese plate in front of him.

The kid had the sense to look abashed, observed Rylie. Luke simply nodded at him and stroked his goatee.

Regan ushered his crew out the door while giving Rylie and the council one last jab.

"At last, we'll have some justice around here," Regan barked. "Jeff will be standing guard until we're ready for you." He smiled and slammed the door shut.

"Quick! Let's block the door!" Imogen jumped up, with Eve behind her. They dragged a chair and upended a coffee table to form a barricade.

Then the shouts and bangs began.

"They must be attacking council chambers," Luke said with a frown. "They're trying to take control of the administration centre."

"Ha! No chance of that!" Kate said. Colour had come back to her face since the insurrectionists left the room. "Those folks are fighters! They're loyal to council and our support of the survivors. They never liked Regan with all his bullish demands to have them repatriated to the mainland."

Kate ran to the window, her belly wobbling over her trousers. "Oh no! Oh NO!" she cried.

"What is it?" asked Imogen.

"They're beating them! They've dragged staff out of council rooms and they're beating them!"

They rushed over to join her. There were a dozen young men struggling with a few council staff. They grappled and shoved. Punches flew, sticks rained down, blood sprayed.

The council team ducked at the sound of a window shattering. They lifted their heads to see a few of the tussling mob tear away and hide behind a nearby building.

Sticks flew and clattered against cabins. Cries sounded as a few more makeshift weapons struck home. One hit their window, and it smashed into fragments over them.

They screamed and moved away. Quickly, they assessed each other for injuries. Luke had sustained the worst of it. He had a shard of glass sticking out from his shoulder and blood streaming down his forehead.

"Luke, get over here." Imogen took control of him. In a flurry of efficiency, she removed the shard as Luke grunted with her ministrations. She grabbed a napkin from the dining table, dabbed at his scalp, and bandaged him as best she could.

"Just a flesh wound," she said. "You'll live."

"Your compassion is overwhelming," Luke said with a wince.

"I can turn it on when required," Imogen said. He smiled weakly at that.

They sheltered now behind the couch, away from the door and the large window with its view out to the main square. Rylie's daughter Eve looked belligerent as ever.

"Mum! Do something!" Eve hissed at her.

Rylie wiped her mouth with the back of her hand. There was a bit of rib sauce there and she licked at it. It spurted some much-needed saliva into her parched mouth. She took a few steadying breaths to settle the tremble in her hands. Eve was right. What they needed now was fearless leadership. She glanced at the faces of her colleagues. Words were cheap. Actions counted. That's what Imogen was always going on about. Too late now, she thought. Regan and his thugs were filling the void they'd left.

Rylie had tried – oh how she had tried! When Maja

Garcia had nominated her governor for this first year of the Terra Blanca experiment, she'd known it was a huge opportunity. It was a fresh start. A second chance. She didn't want to blow it. Not least because she had Eve to look out for. And they had nowhere else to go.

Rylie chanced a peek out the window. One of Regan's goons ran past, brandishing a piece of driftwood covered in blood. She ducked again and cowered as another bang shook the cabin. The shock rattled her bones and her heart flitted like a finch in a cage.

What the hell were they doing out there? she thought. Those idiots would destroy all their hard work. The man-made island state and its beautiful buildings were only six months old. And those assholes were beating people! Regan Delarge was tearing down Terra Blanca before they'd even had a chance. Rylie's anger boiled.

I'll smash Regan's head in myself, so help me God!

How the hell had it come to this?

They all took it seriously, this Terra Blanca. All the councillors. All the citizens. They were all determined to make it work. They all felt so fortunate to be there. Terra Blanca citizenship was by lottery, once they'd qualified, of course. And once here, everyone got a fair share. All voices mattered. Opportunities for all. A role and purpose for everyone in this self-sustaining, man-made society. It was a grand start to this brave new way of living and working together.

Then it had started to rupture. The storm ripped out one of the main greenhouses and they'd had to cut rations. This was made worse when the council agreed to take survivors from the mainland and shelter them in the half-finished accommodation. Rylie was surprised by how quickly their vision was undermined when it came to self-protection.

Maybe Maja could help.

"Imo – I'm going to call Maja on the holo in the bedroom," Rylie said. "She might be able to get us some assistance." Imogen nodded in reply. Rylie crawled to the nearby room.

"Finally doing something," Eve snarled as Rylie passed her.

"We'll talk about this later," Rylie hissed back. She had an uprising to contend with. Her daughter's smuggling, and her galling betrayal, would have to wait.

CHAPTER TWO

Maja watched the holo reports from Terra Blancan residents about what looked like a rebellion.

"They just started bashing us. Yelling at us. They wouldn't stop. There's blood everywhere…"

Maja stared at the images, letting the sounds of terror fill her senses. She felt dread pierce her gut.

This wasn't part of the deal.

Terra Blanca was meant to be a shining example of what's possible for human communities. Not another failed utopian experiment. This was a disaster.

And those poor people!

Enough.

Regret would have to come later. Now she was in damage control. Terra Blanca needed life support. Its tattered reputation could sink them all.

"Athena, call Rylie Addison."

"Calling Terra Blanca Governor Rylie Addison now," the A.I. said.

The drawn face of an ageing brunette jumped into the room through the holo.

"Maja. Thank goodness!"

"Rylie, what on Earth is going on there? There are crazy reports on the holos."

"It's Regan. Regan Delarge. He's led a coup."

"What? What do you mean?"

"Regan's taken over the government with a mob from marine patrol and the Vertical Farm. They're running rampant, rounding up objectors and beating anyone who gets in their way!"

"Objectors? Objectors to what?"

"Look, Maja, it would take too long to explain. We need help – we're trapped. They've locked me and the council in my cabin. We need outside assistance to shut this thing down. Send the military if you can!"

"The military! Surely it hasn't come to that? I'm sure if people just calm down, you'll be able to talk it through—"

"Talk? You can't talk to these people, Maja! They're out for blood! Actual blood!" Rylie's eyes were wild.

Rylie winced as a loud bang rattled the surrounding walls. There were shouts in the background.

"I've got to go, Maja – they're coming for us! Send help – now!"

The holo dropped out.

Maja's heart thumped and her hand flew to her throat. She'd picked up Rylie's panic through the holo. She took a deep, steadying breath.

"Athena, send Huw Chan a message. Tell him, Code Delta. And tell him to hurry!"

CHAPTER THREE

RYLIE SHUT THE holo and jammed it in her pocket. She crawled back to the main room.

"Rylie!"

Rylie glanced at her deputy, Imogen. The younger woman's face was smeared with blood from tending to Luke's injuries. "Rylie! We've got to get out of here!" She gestured to Rylie to come nearer.

Imogen was under the broken window. Rylie nodded and signalled to wait. She raised her head again to see one of Delarge's minions standing outside the door with a shovel in hand. There were no weapons allowed on Terra Blanca. But it hadn't been too hard to improvise. The rest of the community's green square was quiet. People must be hiding in their accommodation, Rylie thought. *I hope they're safe.* Anger surged again. She slid down into a crouch and then, when she was sure the guard was looking away, she scuttled over to join Imogen and the others.

"Rylie, I think I can sneak out the dining-room window. If you distract the guard, I'll slip out the back."

"And go where, exactly?" whispered Rylie. "Regan's men are everywhere!"

"If I can get down to the dock, I can take one of the fishing boats to the mainland and get help."

"Don't you think they will have the boats locked down?" replied Rylie. "Too risky. Besides, I've managed to get a message to Maja Garcia. I've still got satellite comms with her holo. I told her to get the military."

"The military! But that contravenes the Terra Blanca charter. We're self-governing. An island state. The Canadian military can't intervene!" Imogen said, surprised.

"They might when the holos of the insurrection get out. Maja said she saw them on the news report. Someone's managed to stream coverage. There will be news drones and satellite views all over this place. Here, let me show you." Rylie pulled out her holo and pressed the streaming button. Nothing happened. She checked the power – fully charged. She pushed the transmit button – nothing. Damn! Comms were down. But how? She had just used them with Maja. They were supposed to have guaranteed satellite uplink.

"That confirms it, Rylie. We're on our own. Let me sneak out. I can assess the situation. See if I can get to the Innovation Centre and rally a council force."

"Too dangerous, Imo. They're beating people out there! I don't want you hurt. Stay here. We can talk them around," Rylie said.

Imogen's mouth hardened. "Talk is exactly what we don't need, Rylie. Talk is what got us stuck here in the first place. We let the talk go on too long! We needed to take action and now we're holed up in your cabin. Well, I'm sick of waiting and hoping. We've got to do something. People need us. I'm going now – with or without your support." Imogen pushed Rylie away as she tried to grab her hand.

"Imogen – Imogen! Wait!" Rylie cried. Imogen turned back. Rylie looked at Imogen's determined face, then at the dour expression of her daughter. Rylie chewed on her bottom lip, then steeled herself and took a deep breath. She knew what had to be done now. "I'll go. I'll do it. I'm the governor. You stay here. Keep everyone safe. I'll head to the comms tower and try to get it going."

Imogen nodded, and Rylie crawled over to the window. She raised her head carefully over the sill to look out. Then she wound the lever as far as it could go, pulled herself head first through the opening, dropped to the ground outside and was gone.

CHAPTER FOUR

Huw Chan hurried into the room where Maja stood beside the small, round meeting table.

"Maja, I got your message. What's happening? I've seen the holos of Terra Blanca."

"Huw." Maja rushed to meet her business partner and gave him a quick hug.

"I managed to speak with Governor Addison briefly as soon as I saw the reports. She seemed to be under siege. But I haven't been able to raise her again. Comms have all gone dark there. Nothing in or out."

"Have you sent a drone?"

Maja nodded. "It's very strange. There is clear footage all around the island, but nothing when pointed at the island, no matter the distance or angle. It's like some sort of weird comms shield."

Huw tugged his earlobe. "I've heard of that kind of

tech. One of my old colleagues was telling me about it being developed. Very useful for covert military stuff."

"How did any Terra Blancans get their hands on that kind of tech?"

"We clearly didn't screen our residents closely enough. Someone obviously has some serious black-market contacts."

"In any case, Rylie asked me to send military help."

"Rylie asked for *military* support?" It was Huw's turn to be surprised.

"Yes." Maja's voice was dark.

"But that's against the terms of the governance agreement. They are supposed to be self-managing." Huw paused as the reality of the situation sunk in. "Can we even do that? Ask for military support, I mean?"

"I presume so. Like a nation asking for support from its allies."

"To suppress an insurrection."

"It looks that way," Maja said. She sat down and rubbed her forehead.

"Maja, this is a disaster. Our first community needing outside assistance for law and order. It hasn't even been a year!"

"I know."

Huw sat beside her. "What are we going to do?" His face wrinkled with anxiety.

"We need to get them help. I'll call the premier and explain the situation."

"I'll arrange media comms. There is going to be a huge fallout." He pulled his holo from his jacket pocket to make a call. Maja put a long-fingered hand on his.

"Huw. There's something else you should know."

CHAPTER FIVE

RYLIE CREPT ALONG the edge of the accommodation buildings. She could hear the shouts from the uprising coming from the main central platform. What was their plan? she wondered. They'd secured the council members and the central leadership was now off-line. Except for Jerome. Unless he was in on it? That would explain a lot.

Regan's gang seemed to consist of the marine security unit, so all of the boats would be locked down. They would have to try and secure the comms tower if they wanted to eliminate any outside interference.

Rylie dashed to the edge of another accommodation building and paused to listen. She could hear Regan's voice shouting orders for people to stand down. She heard someone running out the front of the building, down the main accommodation access, and she flattened herself into the shadows as best she could.

Who else was part of this? Not everyone disapproved

of the survivors, and the survivors themselves would not be part of the protest. Maybe she could garner some support from them? But their accommodation platform was on the other side of the island. There was huge anti-survivor sentiment among the greenhouse workers and farmers. The aquaculture crew were more amenable to the newcomers since a lot of them had volunteered to assist with harvest and do the dirty work of barnacle-removal and fish-gutting.

Regan and his crew would likely have to lock down the marine harvesting dock to reduce any objections from that cohort. She wondered if she could get to them first and alert them. First, she had to get off her own accommodation platform and skim around the edge of the central community hub without being spotted by Regan's group.

She slipped from building to building without seeing any of them. She also didn't want to alert any of the residents to her presence. There might be some of Regan's supporters among them. Rylie racked her brain, trying to remember who advocated for the survivors and who was against. And where they lived. There were also the objectors, the folks who were against the security protocols that Regan had imposed. Visits to Terra Blanca were already banned because of the pressure on infrastructure and bio-security risks. They claimed that being blocked from leaving the island to crack down on smuggling made it feel like a prison.

Plus, people were sneaking additional resources anyway and adding weight to the accommodation platforms, putting island safety at risk.

Regan's aggressive clampdown on smuggling had only encouraged the black market. Since all official trade was on the Terra Blanca blockchain, people were likely selling work shifts in exchange for smuggled supplies. Or using one of the other blockchain currencies. And to think Eve was part of that! Eve did have the contacts from their time inland. She knew all the food suppliers across Quebec. But what was she using as currency off-island? She didn't have a digital service to offer mainlanders apart from journalism. What else could she use to fund a smuggling operation? Rylie couldn't believe she had been so blind to this.

Rylie stood behind the last building at the head of the bridge to the central community platform. None of Regan's crew were guarding it yet. This was her chance. She took a deep breath and sprinted as fast as she could across the walkway and dived into the shadows on the edge of the parkland that ringed the main island platform. She paused and looked around. Still no sign or sound of the rebels. They must have secured the central hub and moved off to ensure the other industrial platforms were locked down as well. She had to get to the comms centre as quickly as possible.

Rylie scurried from shrub to shrub, staying in the shadows as much as she could. She considered her options. If she did see someone, she could dive off the edge of the platform and swim, but she was a slow swimmer and they could catch her easily. Best to stay on the island platform for now. She could always jump in the water to hide if she thought they were going to surprise her. She kept one eye on the coast as she dashed along the side, seeing if there was an unsecured watercraft. Maybe a personal kayak that had been tied up and forgotten about. Her heart was still pounding and she could feel sweat running down her back. Damn Regan! How had it come to this? Surely they could have talked through the issues without it escalating to violence?

Rylie kept moving, desperately looking for a boat along the shore. But the Terra Blancans had become fastidious about locking up their personal crafts with all the crackdowns on smuggling. They didn't want their boats taken for nefarious purposes. Or confiscated.

Rylie bit her lip at the thought of her own daughter being discovered as one of the smugglers. The gall of it!

How could Eve turn against her?

She shouldn't be so surprised. Ever since they'd left their home, and Eve's boyfriend, the resentment had grown. First shock, then pleading, then vicious criticism.

Rylie became, for Eve, the embodiment of everything that was wrong with the world. Terra Blanca was a privileged and elitist refuge, and Rylie was Gaia Enterprises' willing co-conspirator.

"It's not egalitarian, Mum," Eve had yelled at her as they made their way from the small farming village to the dock on the Fleuve St Laurent. "It's a haven for the privileged few. What about all the other people? They're stuck in climate refugee camps."

True. There were climate refugees everywhere. It was unfair. Terra Blanca couldn't save everybody. But if they could get the community to work, they had a path forward for rebuilding lives.

But that didn't help Jared, his family, or a broken teenage heart.

God save me from the righteous indignation of the teenage soul, Rylie thought. She could understand the passionate despair of young love. Hell, she had had her fair share of tragic love stories. But Eve's resentment ran so, so deep.

A man in maritime patrol uniform came round the corner. Rylie dived behind a shrub. She tried to control her breathing as her heart hammered. Stay still, she thought as she wrestled with panic. She was grateful she was wearing dark clothes. The man was obviously doing a perimeter check. But he was looking out to the water instead of at the building. Small mercies.

She felt the coolness of the evening. Dew soaked into her shirt and trousers as she lay there, waiting for him to pass. Somewhere an owl hooted. But there weren't owls on Terra Blanca. A signal, perhaps? She pressed herself further into the ground.

There was still room in her survival-focused brain to appreciate the grass and plants they had nurtured on their man-made refuge. She breathed in the earthy goodness of the grass. She just wanted to stay there and hide. She squeezed that thought from her consciousness and took a deep breath, pushed herself upright and sprinted the remaining distance to the walkway of the comms tower. This was it. She had to get the comms back up and running if they were to have any hope of salvaging Terra Blanca.

PART TWO

CHAPTER SIX

Three months earlier

Rylie strode across the "green" plaza. Summer blazed, and the grass crunched lifeless underfoot. The lawn needed fresh water, and the irrigation system struggled to keep up. *I must remind Kate to check it again*, she thought. Rylie headed towards the large dome at the epicentre of the Terra Blanca island. Officially, world designer Maja Garcia called it the 'Governance Arena.' Rylie remembered how Maja's beautiful brown face crinkled in delight as she gave Rylie the official tour at the start of her tenure.

"It serves as amphitheatre, entertainment arena, and governance hub." Maja's long, slender fingers swept before her, presenting her work of art. The building was a mini stadium with a glass roof that changed tint according to the weather to allow for views to the sky at night when it was cooler. The entrance was at ground level, with rows of benches leading down towards a central circular platform, like arenas of old. It meant that the central stage was below ground.

"I think of it as a nest. All good decisions can be nurtured here," Maja said with a warm smile.

More like an egg, thought Rylie. A boiled one. She found the building claustrophobic, despite the luminescent dome. All those benches looking down on them. This was where council met, fully in the open, at the bottom of the "nest", at a family-sized round table made of solid oak.

Maja's eyes had gleamed when she walked down to it with Rylie that first time. It was magnificent.

"True craftsmanship," said Maja as she ran her hand over the wood, tracing the intricate trim along the edge. Rylie inspected the carvings: tiny owls linked by vines. "I had Luke Finnegan make it. He'll be joining council as Head of the Wellness Centre."

Luke Finnegan. He was good value, thought Rylie. He was quiet and thoughtful. And a talented woodworker, it seemed.

Rylie's reverie paused as she stepped into the Nest, as it had unofficially become known, feeling the cool breeze of the air conditioning system wash over her. She spotted a lone figure at the round table below. It was Luke, waiting as usual for the others to arrive.

All Terra Blancans were welcome to attend and observe. To challenge business, if they wanted. Council meetings were well attended at first. But it had been spring, and less hot. Plus, all council meetings were streamed and recorded so, if they were curious, people simply watched on their holos. It was mostly procedural except for the occasional heated discussions. Generated by Regan Delarge every time. Every. Single. Time. Or, at least, that was what it felt like. Rylie glanced around, relieved to find he hadn't arrived yet. But he would.

While council meetings were not popular, Terra Blancans did come out for performances. The Nest served as an entertainment centre with VR extravaganzas. The Innovation Centre also ran demos of its latest humanoid robots called Dopplebots. Maja had cut a deal with the founders to run their tech business on the island as part of the Terra Blanca economic incubator. They sold it to the community with guaranteed accommodation berths for the owners and their families on each residential platform, on Terra Blanca and future man-made floating communities. This had made people grumble. Where was the equity in that arrangement? Nonetheless, the Innovation Centre promised to be the economic future for Terra Blanca, selling robots to mainlanders, along with excess food from the greenhouse, aquaculture harvests and insect protein farm. The Dopplebot demos were celebratory moments for the fledgling community. Everyone clamoured to see which celebrity was being brought to life as a robotic doppelgänger.

The oak table maintained its pride of place in the Nest except during performances or Dopplebot demonstrations. Rylie recalled how delighted Maja had been to show her design prowess. She'd ushered Rylie to a small control panel near the first row of benches, pressed a button, and the platform shuddered and groaned. The round table shook and then sank underground. A wooden floor slid over the top.

"The mechanism is a little glitchy," Maja said. "Can you get Kate to take care of that?"

"I'll add it to the list."

Maja gazed up at the amphitheatre and its rows of wooden benches peering down at them.

"From governance to performance – a true arena!" Maja said.

"Perfect for all blood sports," Rylie added.

"Now, now! Governing has its challenges, as you well know, Rylie. But I have faith in you."

Rylie remembered how her face had drained of blood. It was the same old dread sucking her dry. She did know about governing. She had been councillor for a small rural town when the Great Heat had arrived. Crops had dried up, forests burned to cinders, and one by one, the local businesses had closed and people had left. Her heart wrang dry with grief, but she and Eve had stayed, holding out hope for the town. Rylie had kept apologising, trying to reassure the others of a positive future. They had looked at her silently with sunken eyes dim with despair and just shaken their heads.

But in the end, they too had packed up. And that's when Rylie had seen the notice about the Terra Blanca lottery. Maja had picked her out of the applications and offered her the job as governor. She had also given Rylie a tiny owl necklace as they had stood together beside the oak table. "I'm sure you and the rest of the governance council will make wise decisions. I'm counting on it. But just in case, this little guy might remind you of your path."

Rylie touched it now out of habit as she descended the steps to the bottom of the Nest. The usual oppressive atmosphere clung to her. Memories of the last three months rattled like a jar of needles inside her skull. Every meeting was a struggle. Trying to keep everyone happy. Following the pedantic process of collective decision-making. Ensuring fairness for all. Sometimes it was rewarding. Those moments seemed few and far between these days.

Regan was the biggest challenge. He had an opinion on everything. Especially when it came to border control and bio-security. Rylie bristled at the thought of the large man's arrogant pout. His presence was like the prickle of wool on a hot day.

Thank goodness for Luke. He was a reassuring island of calm in the chaos.

"Good morning, Luke," she said.

"Governor," he said as he smoothed his neatly trimmed goatee. "Are you ready for the rumble?"

"As ready as I'll ever be."

They watched the other council members stream down from the entrance. And there behind them, the towering figure of Regan Delarge.

And so it begins again, Rylie thought.

The council meeting proceeded without incident. Quite banal even, thought Luke. He was back in the Wellness Centre to lock up.

Luke sprayed the exercise bike with sanitiser and followed with a cloth. He liked the smell of antiseptic and its astringent tang. Closing time at the Wellness Centre was his favourite time of day. A sense of a job well done, goals achieved. Cleaning up felt like putting things right, imposing order in his small corner of a chaotic world.

The physicality of cleaning helped him push through

the onslaught that came with every twilight. He felt it as a tingle. The pull for a drink. Just one beer. Every day, the vision was as vivid as it had been thirteen years ago. The cap twisting off with a bite into his fingers, the pressured air escaping in a satisfying hiss. The cool refreshing swig, the fizzing bitterness. The droplets of water that formed on the bottle and loosened the label. His mouth salivated.

Luke kept spraying and wiping. That's how you do it. One moment at a time.

He turned his mind instead to the greater task; it was time to make his move. For three months, he'd taken the measure of each of the council members. They were diligent. Keen. Trying hard. He looked for cracks. Little dribbles of doubt and frustration he could use to his advantage.

Kate Watkins was a malleable whinge-pot. Competent enough in managing infrastructure but quick to complain. About everything. Imogen Bussle was a firecracker. Now here was a woman on a mission. She could single-handedly drive Terra Blanca's success as a self-sustaining, man-made community. He admired her tenacity. Rylie was an interesting choice by Maja Garcia for governor, thought Luke. Big on inclusion, shy of conflict. Definitely a weakness he needed to manage there.

The whole Terra Blanca concept was such a good idea. People were excited. It was good news, finally, among all the climate change disasters. A way humans could survive now that the mainland was mostly too hot to live on. Building floating new worlds along flood-ravaged coasts gave climate refugees a bit of hope. Somewhere to go. But more than that – a place where they could build lives, communities, based on great, human-centred principles.

A place to start over.

Luke had followed the progress of the Terra Blanca project from the beginning. Governments heralded Gaia Enterprises as the solution: a new kind of habitat in an over-heated world. Maja Garcia and her co-founder Huw Chan became world design megastars.

He'd asked early for the role as Head of the Wellness Centre, though it wasn't the done thing. He'd had to apply for a lottery ticket, like everyone else. The gig was right up his alley, though. As an organisational psychologist and fitness enthusiast he could implement plenty of powerful programs. He counted on his charm and expertise to sway the scales a little in his favour.

It worked.

Now it was up to them and the Terra Blanca citizens. They would make a new example for human cooperation.

Then Luke got the call. Did he want to be part of the grand human experiment? Did he want to make a difference?

His secret employer wanted him to test and monitor the system as a special agent. There might be weaknesses that some could exploit. As an org psych, he found this a brilliant opportunity for a case study. Could Terra Blancan process withstand leadership challenges? As an insider, he was perfectly placed to test and observe.

Now it was time to turn up the heat.

CHAPTER SEVEN

AT THE NEXT council meeting, Luke was poised to put the pressure on. Along with a handful of staff, they were all here: Rylie, Kate, Imogen, Jerome, Regan. And the usual 'observer': Rylie's daughter, Eve. Rylie's biggest critic. The governor was struggling to handle it. She winced any time her daughter spoke.

Luke got ready to make his move, but it was Regan Delarge who spoke first.

"Governor, Council, I would like to propose an improvement to process."

"Yes?" asked Rylie.

"I think administration is excessive and we have a few superfluous positions. The community is becoming a little top-heavy." The room stirred like a dragon waking from slumber.

Rylie raised an eyebrow and gestured for Regan to continue.

"We're shorthanded in security. People are doing double shifts to handle the load. We've found a number of contraband shipments stashed on the Terra Blanca main hub, but don't have enough resources to both monitor the shoreline and investigate. And in my view, we don't need as many people to 'process' council business." He signalled air quotes. "The A.I. records it all and could handle the reporting and comms, if we delegated more effectively." The jibe was clear and Rylie's face flushed. Her assistants bristled. They were clearly the 'superfluous' positions he was aiming to axe.

Rylie rubbed her forehead and opened her mouth to reply but Regan continued.

"I'm really concerned about bio-security. If just one weevil gets in it could destroy our main grain supply and reserves." The big man's voice chipped at the room and more than one council member moved uncomfortably in their chairs. He was like a broken record. They'd heard it all before. And though they knew he was right, it was always the bad news story of the day that dragged them down.

"We need to clean house. We cannot abide smugglers, people who flout the rules. People who think they are exempt from regulations. They endanger us all. There are plenty of law-abiding, deserving people off-island, in climate refugee camps, who would make upstanding citizens. Frankly, I find it appalling that people would abuse the privilege of being part of this community." Regan sat back in his chair, his bulging arms crossed against the expanse of his chest.

Luke looked over at Regan. This was a surprise. Regan was usually more subdued in council. Bubbling under the surface, but contained. Regan worked hard as head of security, on the water and patrolling the floating platforms. He was used to being outside. Luke noticed how the man often seemed uncomfortable in the room. His body strained against his clothes, as if he had dragged the sky in with him and it was clamoring to be let out again.

Rylie's voice quavered as she replied. "Thank you for your concerns, Regan. Let's work through the process. Each of you can ask questions for clarification. Kate, will you start, please?"

"You bet. First, while I appreciate Regan's bio-security concerns, I don't think we need to 'clean house'. That sounds just a little too draconian."

"I call it as I see it." Regan shrugged.

"I think you're being deliberately heavy-handed to serve your own interests and it's inappropriate," Kate said.

"How is protecting Terra Blanca independence and food security heavy-handed and serving my own interests?" Regan was incredulous.

"Come on, Regan. We all know that you have family offshore you've been wanting to get on the island since we set up here. It would be very convenient to expel a smuggler or two and let your people in."

"Are you saying I'm *staging* this?"

"It's all right, Regan. No one is saying you're staging it," Rylie interrupted. "Your ferocious defence of Terra Blanca, and adherence to our community rules, are well-known. If anything, you err on the side of over-caution. In any case, back to process. Kate, did you have a question for Regan?"

"Yes. Yes, I did. What is it about administrative workers that you find so wasteful? Is it the endless hours they spend ensuring all the people of Terra Blanca receive – and understand – our decisions? The time they spend replying to citizen inquiries? Or the extra hours they spend processing complaints?"

"There wouldn't *be* complaints if people followed the rules," answered Regan. "With more people on security we could resolve the black-market issues that threaten this island and we could get this community properly humming. Fewer people swanning around serving tea in council chambers, more people doing meaningful work." Regan was getting worked up now. Kate fumed.

Luke was surprised by this interaction. He wondered if Regan was not, in fact, another of his employer's plants. He tried to catch Regan's eye but the other man was holding Kate's gaze with a scowl. If he was an agent, he was good, thought Luke. *This is ruffling feathers.*

"You've sure got an opinion on everything, Regan." Imogen sparked up. "Just because people aren't stalking around doesn't mean they aren't working hard. Show a little respect."

"Order! I'll remind councillors that questioning round is not for attacks. It is for fact-finding. Now, if you please, let's return to more civil discussion." Rylie regained command. She went around the room and each of them asked questions. Then they worked the solutions.

"Look. It comes down to this," Regan said, as he jabbed a giant finger on the table like a stumpy drill bit. "We need to shift workers around. Once we clamp down on smuggling, we can get the community back on an even keel. When we look at it, the smuggling might be because food production is lagging. We have failed to meet targets."

"Hey, now," Jerome spoke up at last.

The man was the epitome of relaxed, thought Luke. His limbs were draped like noodles over the table.

"Sorry, Jerome, but you know it's true. We've been on restricted rations for the last month and the lab-grown meat is not keeping up at all."

"That's true. But you just said that smugglers were bad apples. Even if we did boost production, and I'm not saying no to more workers, by the way, how would that stop the black market?"

Regan rolled his shoulders and lay his giant hands flat on the table. "I may have spoken too harshly. Maybe there aren't bad apples. Maybe there are. Maybe the black market would disappear if we got food back to where it ought to be. If I had a few more people on security, we could find out sooner. We can start by culling some of the office service roles and reallocating them to food production for starters. And I could take one or two to help with security."

The room went quiet. They knew all too well the food shortages were problematic. It was the main complaint made to council. Their own households grumbled about undersized carrots, not enough potatoes, and poor tomatoes. Storms had destroyed one of their production units early on and they had been playing catch-up ever since.

"All right, all right," Rylie muttered. Luke watched her shift in her seat and chew her lip. He knew she hated conflict.

This was the perfect moment to prod things a bit.

Luke said, "I propose we examine the administration staffing and look to reassign a portion of each of their working week to food production."

The assistants gasped in disgust at Luke's suggestion. Rylie hesitated.

"That would be fab," said Jerome, and rolled a thumbs-up. "This could be a temporary gig until we can get food harvest back to pumpin'," he added.

"We can also ask if any of the other operational areas could spare workers for a shift each week, too," Imogen said. "It would put Dopplebot production behind, but food is a priority. Also, I can ask two of my programming team members to help with your investigation, Regan."

He nodded at her, his big face brooding.

"Are there any challenges to this proposal?" Rylie looked with reluctance at each of them. "All in resolution?" Hands went up in approval. "Motion carried." Rylie stretched her neck from side to side and rolled her shoulders. "On to the next order of business."

Luke tuned out as he reflected on the tension. The process and Rylie's leadership had survived this challenge. But the divisions were growing wider. Kate was openly hostile and Regan was suddenly a volatile, aggressive change agent, and not just a needling nuisance. Was he a plant or not? Interesting. He'd have to watch and see. Too dangerous to ask and reveal his hand just yet.

Luke sipped at his water and pretended to engage with the discussion around community housing: the heat was stifling, and the ventilation systems were struggling again. Heat made people less tolerant of one another. Food was the uniting force. They all wanted that to improve. Could it also be a weapon to divide?

He turned his mind to the next challenge to council's business.

❧

Luke wandered back to the Wellness Centre, deep in thought. The Terra Blanca employment structure was coming under pressure now. Would it hold up?

His mind re-set as he opened the door. He enjoyed the Wellness Centre. He liked the clean lines of fitness equipment, and their promise of redemption, of righting past wrongs. Each day a fresh start.

But it was more than just fitness here. It was the whole gamut of well-being. Meditation, mindfulness, health assessments as proactive preventatives rather than reactive "health" care. Which was never really health care anyway, he thought. It had been sickness care. They'd turned that on its head here. Each Terra Blancan received quarterly checks: bloods, measurements, the works. They began with DNA profiles, of course. Then each person had their diet and exercise regimen carefully crafted for optimal health. And if there were any nasty latent disease genes, they could edit those out, too.

Yes, Terra Blanca was to be a bastion of health and wellness.

If we can survive the systems challenge.

The door opened and Luke felt the hot air of the day rush in like a furnace blast. George Delaware, one of his trickier patients. He was a short, stout man with thick-rimmed glasses who moved as if he had a walrus strapped to his front. He'd been overweight his whole life, he confessed to Luke, but somehow he'd not yet grown accustomed to his bulk.

"Delaware!" Luke clapped the shorter man on the back

and ushered him to have a seat in the private consulting room.

"What can I do for you today?"

Delaware settled on his chair, his flesh wobbling like custard in a cup.

"I've been getting headaches. Not sleeping well."

"Is that so? Drinking enough water?"

Delaware nodded.

"Have you been doing the movement therapy we talked about?"

Delaware glanced away.

"Some."

Luke considered the man. Some people were tough customers. They knew what they needed to do, they just couldn't break through the years of inner torment to get it done.

Delaware removed his glasses and pinched the bridge of his nose.

"How's work? You're with the Innovation Centre, is that right?"

Delaware nodded and sighed.

"Are you enjoying it?"

Delaware rubbed his pant leg, smoothing a crease.

"I wouldn't say *enjoying* exactly. I mean, I love the work, don't get me wrong. Robotics is something I've loved since I was a kid, you know? Plus the Dopplebots – wow, what a project! It's like bringing back the dead. All the geniuses who could live again. It's amazing."

Luke watched Delaware clean his glasses with the tail end of an untucked coffee-stained shirt.

"It's just... Well, it's just that..."

Luke waited. He knew these moments. These confessionals were the dark thoughts that haunted sleepless nights. We punish ourselves for having them. The thoughts grow louder and louder in our own minds until we fling them into the light. Finally pettiness and horror are made legitimate by giving them a voice. And here was George Delaware on the edge of his own truth.

"It's Imogen."

Luke's eyebrows shot up.

"She hogs the projects. She doesn't let anyone else present at the demos. It's like the Imogen Bussle Show, as if she produced it all on her own."

"I see," Luke said after a moment.

"I'm sorry, you're on council. You've got work with her. I shouldn't have…"

"Not at all, not at all," Luke said thoughtfully. "Tell me, George, are there any examples you can share? Something more specific?"

"Oh, yeah. I suggested we could add supplemental modules to the Dopplebots, such as dialling up humour, or enthusiasm, or firmness. So they stay the same character, but we could add a layer of energy to amplify them a bit, depending on the customer's preferences. This would make it more palatable to the families who own the Dopplebot source materials. Not many of them want AI augmentation and prefer their loved one to stay as they were. More recognisable that way. But if we amplify characteristics that are already latent in the source code, then we get a more interesting, a more tailored Dopplebot, without losing the original."

"Sounds brilliant," Luke said.

"Exactly!" Delaware put his glasses back on and look pointedly at Luke.

"What happened?"

"Imogen asked me to write the amplification program, so I did. She presented it to one of our customers who absolutely loved the idea."

"And then?"

"And then – nothing. No thanks. No appreciation. We're just Imogen Bussle's coding minions."

"Have you tried talking with her?"

"Yeah, right. You know Imogen. She can't sit still for two minutes. Always in a damned hurry."

"Are there others who feel this way?"

"Pretty much the whole coding team."

"That's not good."

"Yup. Probably why I'm not sleeping much these days."

"Probably."

Luke drummed his fingers on his chin and stared up at the ceiling. His eyes narrowed and he found a stray beard hair to smooth.

"So, George, what would you like me to do?"

"What? I don't know. Try talking to her?" Delaware looked hopefully at Luke.

"I'm not in the business of telling my colleagues how to run their teams, George."

Delaware sagged in his chair.

"But here's what I suggest. You and the other coders should discuss it with Imogen. Raise your concerns. Refuse to do any work until she hears your concerns."

Delaware's mouth edges drew long.

"Or – move on. Change teams. We've got a need right

now in both food production and security. Imogen was going to ask people if they wanted to change for a while until we get food production up to scratch so we can ease rations."

Delaware leaned back to consider this suggestion. He clasped his hands over his walrus belly and ran one thumb over the other.

"I also know Kate Watkins needs more people in communications," Luke said. "The comms tower has been problematic. Someone like you could take over that entire division and have it running tip-top."

"What's she like?" asked Delaware after he pondered this for a moment.

"Who? Kate?"

Delaware nodded.

"Oh, well, you know. She complains a lot. Mostly about having too much work and not enough people to do it. But she's a decent sort. And she gives credit where credit is due. She likes people. As a leader, she's more about team than task."

"That would be a nice change."

"And you can always go back to the Innovation Centre later. When the program gets back up to full speed and Imogen comes begging."

Delaware grunted and smiled at that.

"In the meantime, I want to see you in here doing your movement plans. And please reconsider the eye surgery. For someone who works in robotics you sure have a strange resistance to technological enhancements." Luke stood and opened the door for Delaware.

"Not everything needs to be fixed," George said.

"Quite right, quite right."

Delaware walked out into the heat. Luke watched him tuck his shirt in and stand a little taller.

So, this was how the system will be challenged, thought Luke. Now is the season of discontent. Let's see what seeds sprout now that they're sown.

CHAPTER EIGHT

"Damn it!" Imogen threw her comms holo onto the Nest's oak table.

"Trouble in paradise?" asked Luke. He was there early, as usual.

"I've just had another request to join food production from the coding team. That's three more in the last three weeks."

"Have you tried talking to them?" he suggested.

"Ha ha. Of course I have." Imogen flicked her hair and then leaned both fists on the table. "I just don't get it," she said. "It's the most pioneering program around. And they want to leave – for kelp cultivation? It doesn't make sense." She stared at the table and then sat down.

"Sounds like a management problem to me," Luke said quietly.

Imogen glared at him.

"Thanks for your concern, Luke. Management is just

fine, thank you." She ran her fingers around the rim of her water glass. "It's that trouble-maker, Delaware. Things started going weird when he started asking for a promotion."

"Oh?"

"Then he asked to be part of the demos. Then he asked to be part of the client presentations. Then he asked to be named as the chief coder."

"I don't remember seeing him do any of the demos. Or hear about him being chief coder."

"Because I said no, that's why. There needs to be consistency in our product presentations – both in-house and to clients. And besides, Delaware is not that inspiring to look at."

Luke made a face.

"Oh, come on, Luke, you know it's true. He's like a balloon on pegs. Looks like he'll wobble and fall over at any moment."

"Your compassion is overwhelming."

Imogen rolled her eyes. "Well, he's not my problem anymore. He was the first to go. Good riddance. Kate can deal with him. He's on the comms tower crew for a few weeks."

"Deal with who?" Kate stepped down the stairs to the Nest.

"George Delaware."

"George? He's awesome!" said Kate.

"Oh, give me a break," said Imogen.

"I am so grateful for the addition to my team, Imo. We are definitely benefiting from your failures."

"What? They're not failures, for Chrissake. We agreed to reallocate my team temporarily."

"You might need to work on your interpersonal skills is

all I'm saying." Kate raised her hands. She pulled her pink shirt down over her waist. The buttons strained as she did so, then the shirt rode up again as she sat down.

"Where's Rylie?" asked Imogen.

"And Regan for that matter," added Kate.

"Perhaps he'll skip today's meeting for once," said Imogen.

"We can only hope," said Kate.

Luke found himself agreeing with them. Regan was an irritant. If he was an agent, like Luke was, then he was a bit of a blunt instrument. All fire and brimstone. No subtlety.

In any case, it was time to make another move. The governor was gaining confidence in her process.

When people grew confident, they got sloppy.

Rylie arrived and murmured apologies for her tardiness. Something about dealing with Regan, who would not be attending the day's meeting.

"Thank the Lord," said Imogen.

"You do know that the recording is activated as soon as someone steps in this room, don't you?" said Luke.

"Yeah, sure. But does anyone actually watch these meetings, anyway?" Imogen said.

"Eve does," Rylie said.

"Your daughter is one big nerd for governance," Kate said.

"She's interested in politics," said Rylie.

"Obsessed, more like. She goes hell for leather on the community intranet on any damn thing!" said Imogen.

"You just don't like what she wrote about your management style," said Kate.

"What – is everyone a critic today?"

"It's time to get started," interrupted Rylie. "Shall we?"

❧

The meeting proceeded with the usual issues. Concern about food production was running high again as the Vertical Farm was not meeting quota, even with the extra resources allocated. The lab-printed meat machine was on the fritz, and accommodation repairs were behind schedule.

"What is wrong with the cooling system in here?" asked Rylie. She flapped the collar of her shirt in an attempt to cool down. She felt the trickle of sweat run between her breasts into the waist of her trousers.

"Yeah, yeah – we're getting to it," said Kate. "Our list of repairs is a mile long."

"Seems like every meeting we have is about how your department is behind schedule," Imogen said.

"Well, Infrastructure is the biggest sector, thank you very much. But at least our comms tower is working well. Thanks to the deserters from Imo's team."

"Excuse me, Governor," Luke said.

"Yes, Luke?" Rylie said. She had stood and gathered her things as they were just about to end proceedings.

"I've got a concern I'd like to raise."

"We're just about to close the meeting, Luke. Issues are meant to be raised at the beginning so we can craft an agenda together. Can it be carried over to the next session?"

Luke made a show of looking uncomfortable and reluctant.

"Probably I need to raise it now. I would hate for things to get worse." That got their attention, he thought. Heads bobbed up from personal bustle.

"All right then, Luke. Please share your challenge and we can decide as a group to resolve it now or adjourn to later." Rylie sat back down again and looked expectantly at him.

She didn't do much to hide her irritation, Luke thought. Good.

He puffed his cheeks and made like he was girding his courage. "Governor, Council, I've noticed that some people… well, they're not really carrying their weight."

"What do you mean, Luke?"

"There are some workers who are shirking. They quit early. They dodge responsibility. They let others do the dirty work. It's not fair."

Silence simmered. Luke knew the word "fair" was spicy. This community was supposed to be built on fairness: a fair go for all, fair distribution of work, fair access to resources and services. They intended to build equity into the community's DNA.

Rylie spoke first. "Can you back up your claims? Are there others who have observed the same?"

"I haven't really checked with others. That feels a little like gossiping." He said it lightly but knew it thrust a barb at her. A little jab at her integrity. Gossiping was anti-social on Terra Blanca. "I have noted a few incidents, though. I'd be happy to provide my notes to the council."

"Is that really necessary?" Heads swivelled to Kate Watkins. Her tone was edgy. She was rattled, thought Luke. Good. A crack he could work at. "This sounds a little like a vendetta," Kate continued. "I mean, why raise it now? At the end of the meeting? Are you just raising dirty laundry? Petty vengeance or something?"

Luke put on his most offended look and started to protest. Rylie intervened.

"Hang on, Kate. We invited Luke to share his concerns, even if it was out of order. Now we will hear him out. Luke, can you load your notes onto the display?"

"Sure." He drew out his comms device and told his AI to show his work notes. The list appeared:

"Friday 21 June, recycling centre: Jeffrey Patel leaves thirty minutes early without notifying anyone.

Saturday, 22 June, recycling centre: Kylie Sanchez leaves her container-recycling post, asking her colleague Freeda Holz to mind her station. She returns two hours later.

Sunday, 23 June, recycling centre: Jeffrey Patel arrives an hour late, says nothing.

Monday, 24 June, recycling centre: A group of workers leave their posts and spend an hour playing indoor cricket in the processing shed."

A video feed activated and six workers appeared, hooting and hollering while bowling at makeshift wickets. Kate Watkins was one of them.

Kate's face was purple.

"These notes are taken out of context," she blustered. "That cricket game was a bit of tension relief. We just completed a big project. It was reward for hard work, not an excuse to slack off." She gestured wildly.

"I see," said Rylie. "I think this issue warrants more investigation and consideration. If the council agrees, we will defer this matter until we get further information. We might interview the recycling centre staff and see if these issues can be fleshed out. We don't want to jump to conclusions, do we?"

But you already have, thought Luke.

There were a few furtive glances from Kate. Luke made note of them. Little cracks could lead to chasms. He smiled.

"Thanks for giving this some attention," said Luke. "I know it's out of the usual sequence and order of process, and for that I do apologise to the council. It's just, well…" He feigned humility. "It took me a bit of courage to raise this concern. So I'm grateful for your attention."

"And you were right to raise it, Luke. It's important that everyone feels like they have a voice. That issues can be tabled. Now we will give this report due process and make sure we treat everyone correctly."

"I am sure you will, Governor," Luke responded with a thread of sincerity. "You've shown great integrity in all proceedings to date. It's what gave me the courage in the first place."

Wow, he was getting good at ass-licking, he thought. *Should have charged more for this gig.*

CHAPTER NINE

RYLIE SIGHED AS she pulled the door of the cabin shut behind her. She leaned against it and closed her eyes. The smooth, cool surface felt good against her back.

What a day. Luke's concerns had taken a while to resolve.

Rylie and a small citizens' committee considered Luke's complaint seriously and did a thorough investigation. One by one, the incidents were explored. When they reported back to council, every issue was addressed: Jeffrey had left early and arrived late due to pre-arranged hours so he could care for his sick mother. Kylie was absent to fill in for her partner at the childcare centre who was called up for emergency Terra Blanca infrastructure repairs. All absences were approved by the floor coordinator. As for the indoor cricket, people were a mix of sheepish and defensive. Some argued that fun and celebration were integral to happy workers, especially in manual work environments like the recycling centre, and besides which, most of the work was automated.

At the next governance meeting Luke was careful to show gratitude for the investigation. He made a point of apologising to Kate for jumping to conclusions rather than raising it directly with her. His message was clear, though: he was watching her.

Rylie sighed again. Why couldn't they all just get along? It wasn't so hard to just be nice.

She made her way to the kitchen and poured herself a glass of water.

I'd kill for a decent beer, she thought. No one on Terra Blanca had managed to brew anything of merit, and commercial beers were banned along with all other off-shore food items. It went against the self-sustaining food and drink ethos they were striving to create. Plus, as Regan was always droning on about, there was a risk, however small, of bio-security threats. Not that they could get supply from anywhere anyway. What with the droughts, fires, floods and these crazy storms, the food supply chain was under major stress. So, if they were going to drink beer, it had to be brewed on island. They had been allowed to bring wine with their initial arrival. Thank goodness for small mercies, she thought.

She sat at the dining room table and moved Eve's books out of the way. The table was piled high with them. Her daughter had insisted on collecting the printed versions of her favourites. Rylie had argued that it took up a portion of their valuable weight allowance that could be kept for something like clothes or furniture. Eve just stared back at her with petulant defiance. So now *American Gods* by Neil

Gaiman peered back at her. *I'll have to ask about that one*, she thought.

Rylie rubbed her temples. Her head pounded. The heat was getting to her. *Damn that infernal Nest!* It was suffocating.

She took another sip of water and stared at the glass. She could see the reflection of the tattoo on her left inner arm. She pulled back her shirt sleeve so she could take a better look at it. The small image of an eagle, faded to that weird tattoo blue.

"Eagles have the best vision of any animal," Dan had said. Rylie smiled at the memory of her husband. They'd gone together to the tattoo parlour. Matching eagles. "So we'll always have eyes for each other," he'd said.

Rylie rubbed the tattoo absent-mindedly. She remembered the pain clearly.

That and when Dan flew his fighter jet too high, too fast, in training and he blacked out from the G-forces. They told her about it, after. She imagined the plane screaming hard and fast, stalling, then spinning, spinning, spinning until the ground rose up and snatched his eagle from the sky.

"Why do you always do that?"

Rylie startled at the sound of her daughter's voice.

"Eve! You scared me."

Eve sat down across from her at the table, moved a couple of books aside and folded her arms.

"Why do you always let them push you around?" Eve continued.

"What do you mean? Who are you talking about?"

"The council. Regan Goddamn Delarge. All of them."

"Hey, mind your manners."

"My manners are better than theirs! They treat you like crap, Mum. And you do nothing."

"That's not true. We have robust conversations is all."

"Robust, my ass! They complain and complain until you back down and let them have what they want."

"Language! And, not true. We follow process."

"Oh yeah? Did you or did you not agree to let Luke run another investigation on Kate's infrastructure maintenance schedule? Did you or did you not agree to let Regan ramp up security? They're like a militia now. For three hundred people. Did you or did you not agree to let Kate leave an hour early each day this week so she could cool down with a swim?"

Rylie stared at her daughter.

"Have you been doing anything else but spy on council?" Rylie asked at last.

"It's not spying, Mum. Council's business is everyone's business."

"Yes, yes. I know. Haven't you had any studies to do? What are you doing at the Learning Centre?"

"We're tracking the fall of global democracies to autocratic despots. And don't change the subject."

"Sounds like a barrel of laughs." Rylie swallowed the rest of her water in one swig.

"And why are you letting Imogen trial another Dopplebot of Russell McGuee? The last one was like an excited robot monkey. All it did was shout at you and pump the air when you asked it a question."

Rylie burst out laughing, "So it did."

"Well?"

"Well, what?"

"When are you going to stand up for yourself and say no? Regan's nothing but a bully and the others are taking advantage of you being so nice. You don't have to agree to everything, you know. You get to set the standards. You *are* the governor."

Rylie considered her daughter's face. So like her father's. She rubbed the eagle absentmindedly.

"So I am," Rylie said thoughtfully.

CHAPTER TEN

THE NEXT DAY, Rylie met Imogen at the Innovation Centre. They stared at the holo display.

"Are you sure about this?" asked Rylie. "This is really what the A.I. suggests?"

"I shit you not, Governor," Imogen said. "I asked Athena A.I. to give me the best politician that would complement the current council and this is what she suggested."

"But – Vincent Dirk? Really?"

"Yup. Athena considered the current gender balance, experience base, and values set and figured good ole Vincent would level the field for all of us."

Rylie watched the holo display's reel of Vincent Dirk's stats and history. One of the most popular politicians of his time, and a well-loved actor before that. He was known for speaking hard truths with a beguiling smile. It probably wouldn't hurt to help to have more male presence on council. And certainly an A.I. Dopplebot was something new. How will the others react? she wondered.

Damn it, I am the governor. Maja picked me for a reason. Time to make a decision of my own.

"How soon can you have him made up?"

"Give me a week. We'll need to get the skeleton and skin printed. If we decommission the Russell McGuee Dopplebot – for now – we can use his core frame. He's similar in build to Vincent. Then it's just a question of loading all the Vincent comms and data into the processing unit. He'll be a little rough at first – like the Russell Dopplebot. It takes a bit of training and feedback for the embedded A.I. to learn to regulate to its surroundings."

"You've been working on the Russell Dopplebot for a couple of months now. Not much regulating going on there," Rylie said.

"Yeah, but we had thousands and thousands of hours of him in full high octane performance mode. He operated mostly in ninth gear. McGuee was not known for subtlety. His A.I. will get there. I started Athena working with him."

"If we swap out Russell for Vincent, won't this set your program back even more since we reallocated people to food production?"

"Yes. But we've got something more commercial to roll out that will adapt more quickly and be ready for market sooner."

"Oh, yes? Which line are you working on next? Entrepreneurial? Scientific? Artistic? I'd love Michelangelo to come back to life again."

"We're focusing on the governance and politics line. Your request for a politician Dopplebot got me thinking. There will be a huge demand for quality climate governance advice, given the current climate refugee crisis. Places like

Terra Blanca are leading the way, but even we haven't got it all figured out yet. If we tap the wisdom of the past, we might solve our problems faster."

"Who have you picked as your first Dopplebot for the climate governance line?"

"Dr Kiran Beraq."

"Oh! Good one! The family estate released the license? For how many?"

"We can make ten for government Dopplebots and an unlimited number for social good enterprises."

"Fantastic! Will they allow any supplementals?"

"I asked if they would agree to Athena A.I. supplementation and they said no."

"They wouldn't even go for a creativity supplementation? A strategic thinking upgrade?"

Imogen shook her head. "Purist types. I was also looking at Simone Abramowicz but she has a lot less data. Beraq has a lot of comms. We have a ton of writing, audio, and video to funnel into the processor."

"The more you talk, the more you get seen," murmured Rylie.

"So true. Which reminds me, I've been meaning to talk to you."

"Oh?"

"It's about council."

"Oh."

"I think we are getting too bogged down in process. We need to be more decisive. Take more action. Our meetings drag for hours and often deteriorate into bickering. Kate's the worst. She goes toe to toe with Regan at every turn. And what is it with Regan? He acts like he's a bona fide General. The man is a complete bully and you let him walk all over us." Imogen took a breath.

Rylie waited to see if there was more.

"Rylie you're a good governor…"

"But?"

"But the rules are choking the lifeblood out of this enterprise. We need to flex and innovate. Not follow some stilted dogmatic process that was designed by academics, not real people, doing real work, in real situations."

Imogen's words sparked like flint. Rylie felt them burn into her. She swallowed the lump building in her throat. Doubt clouded her thoughts and there was a real danger tears would push through her steely reserve. Did no one back her?

"Thanks for your feedback," she croaked. "I'll take it into consideration."

Imogen eyed her with disappointment.

"Sure. You do that." Resignation laced her voice. "I'll have Vincent ready for Monday's council meeting."

Rylie nodded and turned to leave.

"One more thing…"

"Yes?"

"Who do you want to make Vincent accountable to? Each of the council members?"

"How does that work?"

"Anyone can ask Vincent questions, but only those he is accountable to can get him to move. Command authority, if you like."

Rylie looked again at the holo display of Vincent Dirk with his tall, masculine frame and winsome smile.

"Make him accountable to me. Alone."

CHAPTER ELEVEN

RYLIE WAS LATE to the council meeting on Monday. She had Vincent in tow and wanted to make an entrance. The Dopplebot was huge and lifelike. It trotted behind her like an oversized lapdog.

Luke, Kate, Jerome and Regan stood and balked as the pair descended the stairs to the Nest. Eve was also there in the front row. Rather than watch the recording as she usually did, she had elected to observe in person this time. At the sight of the Dopplebot, she clapped her hands in delight. Imogen beamed.

They stared up at it.

Vincent was sensational.

Rylie savoured the moment.

"So, how does he work?" asked Luke.

"Like our other Dopplebots, he answers direct questions. We can ask him for advice, perspective, or simple observations. He'll come back with a Vincent Dirk-like answer," Imogen said.

"Does he have any enhancements?" asked Kate. "The original Vincent Dirk wasn't known for subtlety."

"We decided not to give him any enhancements," Rylie said. "But we did give him access to Athena A.I. We can ask him to access Athena as part of his response and he will couch it in terms of 'Athena says…' so we know it's Athena talking rather than Vincent."

"Can it actually do anything? Apart from answering questions?" asked Regan.

"His tasks are limited at this stage," said Imogen. "He can walk, sit, nod. He can carry things, like a tray. But nothing more complicated than that. He won't be making any tea, for example."

"But I've always fantasised about Vincent Dirk making me tea! What is your Innovation team doing, Imo?" Kate said.

"You'd have a tea-making Dopplebot if the coding team wasn't being poached left right and centre."

"I didn't poach anyone. They came of their own volition."

"Can it push a broom?" interrupted Regan.

"Can I get him in the Vertical Farm? He's got great reach. It would help a lot with the produce on the top shelf." Jerome looked like he'd just crawled out of bed, Rylie thought. He rubbed his head, stifled a yawn, and tugged the crotch of his trousers.

"How much of a domestic bot is he? Can he do light duties?" Rylie asked to distract herself from Jerome.

"Probably not. No. He's not all that well-balanced. Dopplebots are pretty easy to tip over. It's something we're working on," Imogen said.

"So it's about as useful as tits on a bull, then?" said Regan. "What does it do when it's not being an expensive gas bag with council?"

Imogen ignored the barb and carried on. "We've installed a charging station in one of the council meeting rooms. He powers down while charging. He powers up when asked a question," Imogen said.

"I'm sure we will all find Vincent a really valuable addition to the team," Rylie said. "His experience in politics and his fresh approach will no doubt open our eyes. On many issues. So, without further ado, let me introduce Vincent Dirk, our A.I. Dopplebot, courtesy of Imogen and her team at the Innovation Centre. He will be joining us for council business as a valuable advisor. Vincent, can you please introduce yourself?"

"Hello there. I promise you that I am here to serve Terra Blanca. I will pump up Terra Blanca. We'll make this place great. Others will sing our praises. We'll be the envy of everywhere."

"Okay then," said Luke.

"That's Vincent Dirk all right," Imogen said.

"Thank you, Vincent. It's great to have you here. Now, let's begin. We have a lot of work to do. Agenda items?"

Regan raised his hand slowly, while keeping his gaze on Vincent. Even he looked small next to the big Dopplebot. He puffed his chest self-consciously.

"I'd like to request more workers for marine patrol, please," he said.

"Not this again," Imogen said. "Regan, you've already been given extra people. The council staff have been pilfered several times now. Can't you get on top of it? What are you doing down there?"

"Sweet F.A.," said Kate.

"Ladies, a little decorum, if you please," Luke said. "We have a new member on the team, and we don't want him getting the wrong impression, right, Vincent?"

They looked up at the Dopplebot.

"Impressions. Impressions are cheap. They tell you nothing about real interaction, real engagement," said the Dopplebot.

"Um. Wrong context, Vincent," said Imogen.

"Thank you for the feedback. It helps me learn. I don't have impressions, just analytics."

"Vincent, can you analyse the team so far?" Luke tried again.

"There are three women, three men, and a young female observer. One is bi-racial, one is a lesbian. Apart from that, there is a distinct lack of social, racial, and cognitive diversity on this team. There is also disagreement and tension." The Dopplebot paused and seemed to access something internally. "And there is a sad lack of discipline in the room," Vincent said.

Silence.

Luke cleared his throat. "How about we get back to following process then?"

Rylie's heart swelled. At last! The Dopplebot's presence was cracking the team's patterns. They might just get on with it and start running a smooth operation.

They resumed council discussion and hammered out the terms of Regan's request for additional team members. Two office staff would go on loan until they finished installing the new shelving in the marine patrol storage shed.

Things were drawing to a close when Luke spoke up.

"I'd like to table another matter," he said.

"Yes?" Rylie said.

"I think we need a Communications Officer."

"Why?" Kate asked.

"We're starting to make real progress and we are missing out on valuable positive public relations stories. Look at Vincent, for example. Here's one of our own products that we've adopted for governance. It's a huge story that would help sell our Dopplebot products."

"Excellent idea, Luke," said Imogen. "Thanks for thinking of the Innovation Centre for once."

"Really? You really think we need *more* shiny bums in this place?" said Regan.

"I think it's a terrific idea," Kate said. "We could put it out to the Terra Blancan community and see what they say."

"I don't think that's quite necessary," said Luke. "I think we have the ideal candidate right here." He gestured to Eve, who had been sitting earnestly in the front row as she often did. "She's the most committed attendee and makes very pointed remarks on our message board. She's half doing the job already."

"She's the governor's daughter, Luke," said Imogen.

"With only three hundred people on the island, someone's bound to be related to someone when it comes to new jobs," he replied.

"Eve, what do you think of the idea?" asked Rylie.

"I'd love to!" Eve was perched on the edge of the bench,

squirming with excitement. "Look at the Dopplebot! This is a huge opportunity! I could write a few articles, do an exposé, run a holo livestream of Vincent in action. We could do a ton of stuff." Eve's face danced with delight.

Rylie loved seeing her daughter so positive for once. She glanced over at the Dopplebot.

"Vincent, what do you think?" she asked.

"It reeks of nepotism," the Dopplebot replied.

"That's a little harsh, Vincent," Kate said.

"Thank you for the feedback. It helps me learn. It *smells* of nepotism."

Silence.

Rylie's face flushed and her palms moistened. *Damn the Dopplebot!*

"It's not a good look to appoint your daughter," Imogen said.

"I'm telling you, we don't need another paper-pusher," Regan added.

"I could always use more help in the Vertical Farm. Or in the compost shed," added Jerome. He took a big sip of water, and some splashed down his front. Kate smirked as he tried to pat himself dry. "Damn it!" He pulled the saturated shirt away from his skin, then gave up.

"Perhaps we should put it out to Terra Blanca on a direct vote?" Kate said.

Rylie felt the critiques poke the embers of her temper. Why did everything have to be so damn complicated?

"Nonsense. We don't need to bog the community down with every little thing." Rylie pulled her chair in to the table and leaned forward. "As governor, it's within my remit to appoint additional roles as required. I agree with

Luke, there is a need, and we have the perfect resource. As Luke said, no one else shows as much of an interest in council business. We'll appoint Eve on a trial basis, starting immediately. Regan and Jerome, I hear your concern for more labour, but a teenager is not the solution. If anything, we can ask for a few more hours from each of the other divisions again. Eve, you can start with a profile on Vincent, as suggested."

"Hang on a minute," said Regan. "Don't you think we should run this through council process?"

"No. Thanks for your concern though, Regan, about council process. You may not be familiar with the Charter where it says the governor can make minor ad hoc appointments without full council consultation. This is a minor appointment, on a trial basis, so that's my decision. And we're done for today. Thank you, all." She nodded and beckoned to Vincent to follow her. They marched up the stairs.

"Well, well, well," said Imogen. "It looks like the governor is finally governing."

"If that's what you'd call it," said Regan.

CHAPTER TWELVE

REGAN DELARGE CLAPPED his new workers on the back as they reported for their assignment on the docks for marine patrol. He'd managed to wrangle two more from council after another round of bargaining.

"Welcome! This is where the real work happens, folks!" He beamed at them. They were sullen. "Marty will get you all set up. We've got boat maintenance and cleaning to start. Then we'll check in at the Vertical Farm later this afternoon." He smiled broadly and reached out his arms. "Nothing like honest work in the sweltering sun to feel like you're making a real difference, eh?" The two admin workers said nothing.

He left Marty and the two rookies to get on with the work. Finally, the council had listened to him. These softies would learn that a community needed to toil for its spoils. No one got a free ride here. It was something he'd learned in the long, hard days running his own show. Back in the day, before the pandemics and fires wiped out his farm supply business. Those were long, hard, dark years.

No more. Regan had managed to secure one of the council roles as Head of Security and he was determined to make the most of it. This place had potential. It just needed clear direction. And a cracking whip to set the pace.

He had the docks under control now. His crew was young and keen. He was proud of his boys. And Brenda. She was a doer. A hard worker.

Regan walked the short distance to the Vertical Farm. The building was a tall, green-sleeved, transparent shed that lined the southern shore of their man-made island. It was designed to produce all the food they'd need to be self-sufficient. But damn, he was sick of fish and vegetables. And insect protein. He yearned for meat. It was one of the rules about Terra Blanca that irked him the most. They were supposed to be self-sufficient to make sure their food production was secure. He got that. He agreed with that. But giving up steak? Real steak?

Meat was too expensive on the mainland, anyhow. Land was at a premium with most of it non-arable after fires and floods and the crazy hot temperatures. People and animals were crammed into small strips along the coasts. It was a heaving mess of squalor. No space for animal production. That's why Terra Blanca was so coveted. Everything clean, new, and immune to further sea level rises due to its innovative tethered platform technology.

Damn, he missed bacon! The fake meat pea-protein version was a bastard cousin to the real thing. If only their lab-grown meat could kick into production. They'd had so many food production issues and equipment breakdowns.

It was harder to set up than they had anticipated. At least the aquaculture products were going well. All good if you liked fish and molluscs and kelp. Which he didn't.

And then there was Jerome.

He is as useless as a glass hammer. And that numb-nuts is in charge of food supply!

The Vertical Farm, the insect protein, the lab-grown meat, the fishing – all of it. If Terra Blanca was going to get enough produce to feed them all, let alone sell the excess, he had to get that turd Jerome to actually run the farm properly.

How does such an incompetent get to be in charge of the most important asset of the island? What was Maja Garcia thinking? Plus, that goddamn Governor Rylie Addison had no idea what she was doing. She was too afraid to pull Jerome into line. Seriously. She was a freaking liability.

They should extend his role from island security to food security. He could do a better job than that nitwit, Jerome. Hell, anyone could. Then maybe they wouldn't have such an issue with smuggling. If people had enough good, decent food to eat, that would eliminate a whole bunch of headaches.

Regan pushed the door of the farm shed open and took a deep breath of the moist air. It felt sodden with plant life. The air was lush and cloying. He loved it here. Almost as much as the docks and the thrum of the boats when he was at the helm, riding the watery horizons of the great Canadian north. Agriculture and food production was his real calling, though. Feed the people and all goes well.

Where is that layabout Jerome, anyway?

"Speak of the Devil!" A voice laced with laughter

reached through the rows of plants. Regan spun to see Jerome Gagnon swagger out from the tomato vines. Two flush-faced women chuckled at his side, leaning against one another. An animal-like intimacy snaked between the three. That's a just-been-fucked-face if I ever saw it, thought Regan. They practically reeked of sex.

"Jerome," Regan said. "Ladies." He nodded at them. The taller one put her hands on her hips and tilted her head at him with a salacious smile.

"What ya up to, big fella?" asked Jerome. "Your crew coming soon for maintenance? We've got algae in the tanks again."

"Of course. I told you we'd donate a few hours every day. They'll be here this afternoon. Anything else need looking after?"

"I can think of one or two things…" The tall woman gazed at him intently with an eyebrow raised. Her companion chortled.

Regan looked back at her, deflecting the suggestion with an impassive face.

"Jerome, I was wondering about the lentils. How are they coming along?"

"Not that again! Look, man, I told you I was working on it. We've got the seedlings under the lamps. We're on it," Jerome looked flummoxed.

"Are you, though? You said that a month ago. There was nothing higher than a centimetre when I checked last week."

"I said, we're working on it." Jerome's smile flat-lined.

"Really? Looks like you're working hard on something else." Regan pointed his chin at the two women.

"Hey. That's none of your business," Jerome said. His face was red now. "We get the work done. That's what matters."

"That's just the thing," Regan said as he stepped a little closer to loom over Jerome. "The work is *not* getting done. People are hungry. We're sick of the same old, same old. You promised us crop diversity, fast-growing produce with your fandangled genetic splicer. But so far, it's all just talk."

"Hey, man. Chill out." Jerome took a step back with a placating gesture. "Things are happening. They just take time."

"Whoa now, big fella!" The taller woman pushed between the two of them. Regan felt her breasts graze his chest before she put a hand on his shoulder and turned him away from Jerome. "There's good stuff happening here, Regan. I'll give you a tour. Show you the… ins and outs… if you know what I mean."

For Chrissake, thought Regan. *Do they trade in sex down here, now? A new currency? What bullshit.*

He gave the woman a hard stare. Her mouth tightened.

That threw water in her jocks, thought Regan. *What was she thinking? That I'm some sort of hot-pants neanderthal?*

"Jerome, you and your crew are on notice. This farm needs to ramp up or you're out."

"Oh yeah? On whose authority? You don't speak for council!"

"Don't be so sure about that." Regan's voice was dark.

Jerome waved his arms in frustration. "You're the Head of Security, for crying out loud! Why don't you stick to what you do best – strutting about and looking serious."

"Careful now, Jerome. A man is more than what he

does." He glanced again at the two women. "And for you, Jerome, ladies, that's probably a good thing."

The two women stood with crossed arms and glared.

That will sour their afternoon delight, thought Regan. He left the building and smiled to himself.

Good. Now he had a plan.

CHAPTER THIRTEEN

"Motion resolved," Rylie said. "Regan Delarge will take over management of the Vertical Farm, along with his security duties. Jerome will be redeployed to pest control under Regan's supervision. Council business is adjourned for this week. Thank you, everyone."

Luke remained seated while the others gathered their things and made ready to leave the room. *This is an interesting development,* he thought. *What is Regan up to?*

"This is outrageous!" Jerome stood with arms waving madly. "Governor Addison! You can't let this happen! Regan is out of line!"

Rylie put up her hands to placate him. Luke and the other councillors stopped to watch the outburst.

"Hang on, Jerome. We've heard the reports and seen the video footage. Did you or did you not partake in group sex with two other workers in the seedling cultivation room, after hours last Thursday?"

"That was – that was consensual!" Jerome stammered. "No one's business."

"What you do on your own time is definitely *your* business. But it is definitely *council* business when it happens on community property and risks the health and hygiene of our food source." Rylie's face rippled with revulsion.

Jerome opened his mouth to protest but Rylie continued. "Did you or did you not fail to follow nutrient cycle protocols?"

"That was a technical glitch."

"Did you or did you not fail to deliver the crop quotas – again – in spite of suggestions from others?"

"Regan was just trying to make me look bad. The crops aren't doing great. I know that. We tried lots of stuff. It's not my fault." He eyed each council member for support and received none. Finally, he turned to the Dopplebot.

"C'mon, big fella. You're a man of the world. You know when a guy has been doing his best. I deserve another chance, don't I?"

The Dopplebot moved in front of Jerome with a mechanical plod. "Jerome Gagnon. You're a two-bit layabout. Your dereliction of duty is reprehensible, second only to your unfettered sexual licentiousness. You are not fit for purpose."

Jerome gawped.

Rylie touched the Dopplebot, and it moved aside. "Jerome, you were responsible for the food production for three hundred people. Your behaviour showed a cavalier disdain for the responsibility. You treated the Vertical Farm as your own personal saloon. It's not good enough."

Jerome's mouth sagged.

Rylie continued. "We've all assessed the situation. It seems you are out of your depth here and the kindest thing is to allow you to redeem yourself in a more discreet role. If you master pest control, we can look at management duties again later."

Luke studied Jerome's face. It looked like the man had swallowed a turd. Then Luke noticed Regan leaning against the wall, his thick arms crossed against his enormous chest. A creeping grin of satisfaction crawled across his features.

Delarge, you cunning bastard, Luke thought. *Nothing like loss of status to lay a man low.* If he was testing the system, he'd worked a nice piece of subterfuge here. People don't like public shaming much. It turns them bitter.

But what was his end game?

Rylie was handling the process well, as far as he could see. She had just thrown Jerome a lifeline: the possibility of redemption and a path forward – albeit with a temporary blow to the ego.

Luke thought about this some more. What's deeper than status to challenge a system? Survival threats. Food was the key. If Regan was in charge of the Vertical Farm now, could he make the food shortages worse? Was that how he was going to test the system? But why not just let Jerome continue to falter?

The more he considered Regan's possible plans, the more obscure they seemed to be.

Food scarcity was one challenge. What else might threaten Terra Blanca?

Luke scowled. He felt unsettled for the first time, and he didn't like it.

CHAPTER FOURTEEN

Luke winced as he read the headline.

VERTICAL FARM STILL STRUGGLING: IS SHANE UP TO THE JOB?

Eve's latest critical article took aim at Regan's new second-in-command at the Vertical Farm. She seemed to have the entire new regime in her sights. Since Jerome was ousted and Regan had taken over, Eve had peppered the Terra Blancan community intranet with strident criticism of their work. Somehow Jerome had retained his popularity in spite of his incompetence. This was a mystery to Luke. What was it about that guy that people loved so much?

It seemed Eve had fallen under his spell, too. She seemed committed to having Jerome reinstated. And so she made council her target for getting it done. Eve continued to attend all council meetings, judiciously making notes for her next scathing editorial. Maybe she hoped to criticise them into putting him back in the job.

When Regan raised the issue of Eve's badgering at council, Eve was quick to jump in.

"It's called free speech, dude!" She smirked at him.

Regan's ice-blue eyes held her gaze as he pursed his lips and breathed heavily through his nose.

"Perhaps you'd like to come down to the Farm and work alongside the guys for a day. Get a sense of what real work is like."

"Can't be too hard if that dipshit Shane Johnson can do it. Oh, yeah, that's right, he can't do it. He's an incompetent douche."

"That's really uncalled for, Eve," Rylie said. "It's one thing to write about genuine issues and another thing altogether to be insulting."

"Perhaps a stint down at the Farm would be a good idea," Luke said. "That way no one can accuse you of hearsay. It would be genuine reporting."

"Whatever." Eve flopped back on the bench and scowled.

"You're welcome any time, Miss Addison," said Regan. "I know Shane is keen to show you the ropes."

"I thought we agreed: no kids on the production line," Rylie said.

"If she's old enough to manage comms, then maybe she's old enough to pick lettuce," Imogen said.

"It's just for one day, anyway," Kate said. "I think it might be good – the voice of Terra Blanca getting firsthand experience of our biggest issue."

Eve thought about it for a moment.

"Okay. Yeah. Sure. I'll do it. I'll spend a day working on the Farm. But I'm telling you, I am going to report what I experience truthfully."

"I wouldn't have it any other way," Regan said through gritted teeth.

"I'll go too," added Luke. "To represent council. And make sure our Comms officer is treating her assignment fairly."

"I don't need a babysitter, Luke," Eve said.

"What makes you think I'll be protecting *you*?" Luke winked at Eve.

"Fine," Regan said. "Like I've been saying all along, we don't have enough people to get the job done. I'll welcome any warm bodies if they're willing to work."

❦

Luke and Eve arrived at the Vertical Farm where Regan waited for them.

"Luke, you'll work alongside Shane. You're checking pests and pH levels today. Eve, Marty is going to look after you. You guys are stacking and distributing the latest salad harvest."

Luke nodded to Eve, who saluted as she trotted off behind Marty. Marty's sour face showed how enthusiastic he was about his assignment. They'll have a fun day, thought Luke.

"Hey, Shane!" Luke thrust his hand into the young man's rough palm. "What can I do to help?"

Shane avoided Luke's eyes and mumbled to follow him. Once they were in the Vertical Farm shed, Shane pulled Luke over to show him the issue they were facing.

"It's the crickets. Some escaped from the cricket protein hutches," he said and plucked one of the voracious brown insects from the stem of a cucumber plant. "We've sprayed with a fairly gentle natural insecticide and got most of them, but some are still out there. Without moving to a more toxic insecticide, the only solution now is to pick them out by hand."

"But there are hundreds of these plants!"

"Yeah. Exactly. Just when we get to the end, we have to come back to the first ones because the bugs have jumped."

"All right then. I guess we should get started."

It wasn't long before Luke's back was aching and his fingers were sticky with bug juice. Luke paused and went to grab a drink of water. Shane joined him.

"Is this what Jerome was doing?"

Shane shrugged. "I'm not sure *what* Jerome did, exactly. As far as I can tell, he didn't pay much attention to the bugs. He was happy to just spray everything. If the plants didn't survive, he'd just order the crew to replant."

"Is that why there were so many shortages?"

Shane's mouth quirked at the corners.

"Not for me to say. I only started here recently."

Luke swigged from his water bottle and wiped the sweat on his brow with his short sleeve. He watched Shane try to cool down by pulling his wet shirt away from his sodden wiry frame.

"Hey, Shane. What did you think of Eve's latest article?"

Shane's eyes hardened. He looked at Luke's face for the first time.

"What did I think? I thought was a real bitchy thing to

write. That spoilt brat doesn't know the first thing about what it's like to work down here. To clean up someone else's mess."

Luke stayed quiet and let him continue.

"Regan and us – we're trying real hard. But not everybody takes it seriously. Jerome? He's a freaking joke. He's more busy chasing pussy than doing any real work. But you don't hear prissy Miss Addison writing about that, do you?" Shane picked up a piece of irrigation tubing that was on the floor and twisted it around his fingers. "That guy – Jerome. I don't know what he has about him. He's got a real shlong shield."

"A what?"

"You know. Shlong shield. A cock cape."

Luke looked blankly at him.

"He waves his cock around like it's some sort of magic wand. His dick protects him – like a shield. Chicks just love him."

Luke stared some more at Shane. Then he smiled and said, "Well, if we could all be so lucky."

Shane looked at him in surprise and then smiled sheepishly. Luke punched him on the shoulder and said, "C'mon. Let's get back to work. There's another mile of bugs to catch."

Eve's article came out the next day.

VERTICAL FARM ON SHAKY FOUNDATIONS

Luke groaned. This was not going to go down well.

"I spent a day hustling with Marty Van Hoe down at

the Vertical Farm. He had me running from pillar to post, packing boxes and hauling ass. While he worked me hard and didn't stop for a break all day, he still couldn't hide the fact that the Vertical Farm is failing. It's failing to meet targets. It's failing to stay on top of orders and packing. It's failing to create an enjoyable place to work. Is it just because there is too much work? Or is it because the workers are just not up to it? Take Shane Johnson, for instance. After interviewing his predecessor, Jerome Gagnon, it's clear that Shane just does not know what to do…"

Luke stopped reading. Eve had written an exposé without even talking to Shane. He knew – he'd been there all day with the quiet man. Eve had based her entire opinion on Jerome's sour grapes.

Luke closed his tablet. The real question was what would Rylie do about it? Would council address this undermining? Or leave it as "Freedom of the Press"?

CHAPTER FIFTEEN

"Good morning, Governor!"

Luke found Rylie where he'd hoped she'd be, down by the coastline in a shady spot overlooking the water. It was dawn, before the heat and bugs swarmed the shores. He knew she favoured this spot. It was secluded and did not get much foot traffic from the community as it was a little awkward to get to.

"Ah, Luke. Good morning," she said from her perch on a large, flat rock. "You're up early."

"I like the dawn. It always brings a sense of hope. Like something miraculous might occur. Before the disappointment sets in."

"That's a little pessimistic."

"I like to think it's realistic. Life often fails to deliver on expectations." He stood next to her rock. "May I join you?" He knew she preferred solitude, but this was his chance.

She shuffled over to make room for him. They sat in

silence for a few minutes and looked over the lake. Diamonds sparkled on the water as the flash of the sun's rays eased the dawn into day.

"Governor, I was wondering if we might have a word?"

"What is it, Luke?" Weariness clung to her.

"I'm wondering if we might do something special for the council members."

"How do you mean?"

"Everyone has been working so hard. Dealing with some serious issues. That thing with the Vertical Farm management was tricky. Eve really did a number on Regan and Shane. They've been pretty bent out of shape." Luke leaned over to scratch his leg, waiting for Rylie to say something. She didn't, so he continued. "It might also be time to get Jerome back in his role. When we put Regan in over him, the councillors copped some serious flak from Jerome and his buddies afterwards. And more so from the community. Jerome has been ranting and calling Regan a bully. Everybody seems to be up in arms at the moment."

"I'm aware of Jerome's disappointment. And of the tone of Eve's articles. I am taking steps to address it," Rylie said.

"That's good," Luke said. *She's really on top of this*, he thought. *I wonder if this next suggestion will work?* "In any case, I think council needs a bit of a break. Something nice to reward us. For all the hard work. And for having to deal with the social pressure and all that."

"What did you have in mind?" she asked.

"Nothing big. Like a private dinner or something. Something to say thanks."

Rylie sat with that for a moment.

"I'm not sure that's a good idea."

"Why not?"

"Service is a privilege. It's not *for* privileges."

"Come on, Rylie. There's a difference between a simple 'thank you' and screwing the system. Council is a team too, and all teams need a little appreciation."

She crossed her arms and considered his statement.

"That may be true. And yet public perception can make monsters from mice."

Luke resisted the urge to press the point. He knew if this was going to work, it had to be Rylie's initiative, and not one he pushed on to her.

"You may be right there, Governor."

He picked up a twig and poked at a patch of lichen on the rock between them.

"It's a shame, though," he added quietly. Rylie glanced at him. "So much goodwill in the councillors. I hope it doesn't start to wane. It's a long time before the next appointees take over. A long time for selfless service. Especially if they cop any more fallout from the Jerome situation."

"I'll think about it," Rylie said.

"Thanks, Governor. I would hate for all our hard work to come undone." Luke stood and patted her on the shoulder in farewell. This was a real test, he thought. Gratitude could be a boost. Or it might split them apart.

❧

Rylie walked back to her accommodation and thought about what Luke had said. The councillors had been working really hard. It was a tough gig. And thankless. No matter what you did, people always found something to complain about. It tested the resilience of even the most stalwart of leaders. It might just be time for a special thank you.

Plus, they really needed to build better rapport. So much tension between them, rubbing like grit in a wet shoe.

Rylie entered her home and sprawled on the couch. A quiet moment to herself in her cabin was bliss. It wasn't much, just like everyone else's. Basic. There wasn't much room on Terra Blanca, so the accommodation design was fairly simple. Still, it was comfortable, and it was home.

For the most part Rylie enjoyed the governor role. She embraced the challenge. She wanted to see Terra Blanca thrive, just like everyone else. This was the future of human civilisation. They had to make this work. People were pushed onto smaller and smaller parcels of land, and these floating communities where the way of the future. Humans had to learn how to live, work, and play together in small, contained areas.

Rylie felt something tugging at the back of her mind. She stood and started tidying the living room. Putting things in order always helped clear her thoughts.

Trying to get along was not a new leadership challenge, so why did this feel so different? Maybe because they had so much idealism woven into it. It was a collective. It was decentralised leadership, with the council serving as a coordinating decision maker for whole of community decisions. The council was a citizens' assembly. At least, it would be, after this first governance group that had been hand-picked by Maja. The idea was this first council could establish community process and norms more quickly.

Once the original council had Terra Blanca established and running well, they could incorporate more and more collective decision-making. They needed to ease people into it. Next year, people were to be nominated on a roster for a term to govern Terra Blanca business. Kind of like a jury.

What they really needed was the food production to work. The whole self-sustaining community idea hinged on that.

Rylie ferreted in one of the kitchen drawers for a cloth and returned to the living room. There was a lot of dust that came in, despite it being a floating terrace. It must be from the new accommodation platform being built. That too was behind schedule because the workers were being reallocated to food production at least one afternoon a week. She dampened the cloth and ran it across the few surfaces in the living room and along the skirting boards.

In the meantime, this council was still learning. So far, so good. Apart from the food situation. And the smuggling. And the food import bans. And the personal belonging limitations. When it came to complaining, people weren't shy about expressing their opinions.

She thought about the councillors. There was some flagging enthusiasm. Kate was grizzling about the never-ending list of maintenance items. But then again, she had been cantankerous from the beginning. Imogen seemed more tired than usual. While the Beraq Dopplebot project was going well and they had sold out in pre-orders, the Russell McGuee Dopplebots had hit a snag. The testers complained that its answers devolved into passionate rambling. Though the testers reported being transfixed by its responses, they often forgot the original question by the time the Dopplebot had finished its reply. In android-form as in real life, Russell McGuee had a hard time keeping it short.

Then there was Luke. Thank goodness for Luke. The Wellness Centre was running smoothly. They handled scrapes and breaks, coughs and cancer, all while running preventative diagnostics and all sorts of health programs. It was a thriving hub of social activity, too.

Luke was right. The role of councillor had to have some reward to it. Otherwise, no one would want to be part of the citizens' assembly. They would find excuses to get out of the duty instead of seeing it as a huge honour and opportunity.

So, what could she do as a thank you that wouldn't seem like an elitist privilege? A simple gathering could be the way. No one could hold them as being above themselves if they just shared a meal together. Surely that would be acceptable in the public eye?

The thank-you dinner was a good idea. They could take a little bit of food from the reserves. She'd ask Jerome if they could have something a little extra. Not much. It could work. Nothing too big. Just something nice and little to show appreciation. Surely, they deserved it?

Rylie resolved to organise the celebration. For her, Imogen, Kate, Luke, and Eve, of course. Jerome? Yes, a gesture towards reinstating him. He had actually improved his performance in his truncated role. Plus, that would get the complainers off her back. Regan? She groaned at the thought of him and his steely eyes full of derision.

Perhaps we'll make this one an unofficial gathering. Regan doesn't need to be part of everything.

No, she thought. He's part of the team, even if he is a painful part.

CHAPTER SIXTEEN

"ARE YOU SURE about this?" Imogen asked Rylie. She, Kate, and Luke stood in awe around Rylie's dining table, laden with more food than they'd seen since they left the mainland.

Eve popped through the doorway from her bedroom. "Is that pasta?" She examined a serving bowl loaded with noodles and rich red tomato sauce.

"And cheese! Oh my God!" Kate cut herself a chunk of Parmesan and dropped it into her mouth. She sucked the remnants from her pudgy fingers before hacking off another slab.

Jerome grinned like a stoned baboon as he brought in a bowl of vegetables. "Picked today," he said. "First crop of broccoli." He had taken some of the food from reserves, as requested by Rylie, then added additional supplies from the Vertical Farm as a surprise.

Rylie patted Imogen on the shoulder and nodded to

a chair, suggesting she sit and enjoy. Rylie watched the expressions of delight on her colleagues' faces. Except Luke, who was his usual stoic self. *I don't get that guy*, she thought. *He needled me into this and now he looks like the cat died.*

"What's up Luke?" she asked. "Not to your liking?"

He blinked in surprise and then shifted on his feet. "Not at all, Governor. This spread is – remarkable. Thank you. Well done." He looked like a cat about to cough a fur ball. Rylie waited for him to finish his thought.

"I'm wondering where Regan is."

"He should be on his way. He said he'd come along."

"I see." Luke looked down to gather his thoughts. "And Regan approved the disbursement of the reserve supplies?"

"No, Jerome did. He is still in charge of supply." Rylie's mouth was dry, and she took a swig of water.

"That's…interesting."

"Hey, man, it's all good. We have enough broccoli for everyone. And I only took a couple of jars of sauce." Jerome clapped Luke on the shoulder.

"And cheese. And pasta."

Rylie considered Luke for a moment. *What is his problem? He is the one who suggested this dinner.*

There was a knock and Rylie went to let Regan in.

"Sorry for being late. We were locking up the reserve store. It was left open." He froze. He scanned the table and his cheeks flushed.

"What is this?" he asked carefully.

"It's dinner," Rylie said. "A thank you for all your hard work."

She poured a glass of wine and handed it to him.

"Wine?" His face was incredulous.

"From my private stock. I brought it with us, at the start. I've been waiting for a good time to share." She gestured to a chair. "Please, sit."

Regan stared at the wine and then put it down on the table. He took his seat slowly, with his lips squeezing together in a flat, grey line.

"Here's to good work and dedicated service," she said. "May we all feel truly appreciated."

"May we be truly *grateful*, and mindful of the needs of others," added Imogen. The younger woman looked pointedly at Rylie.

"Yes, of course," countered Rylie, realising she had forgotten the ritual of thanks. "May we be truly grateful and mindful of the needs of others."

"What – the hell – is this?" Regan snapped.

"I beg your pardon?" Rylie said. "It's dinner. It's my way of saying thanks after all the hard work you've done."

"I heard that part," Regan seethed. "I want to know why there's food from the reserves on the table. And why the new harvest is here. And why there is enough goddamn food to feed three families!"

"Hey, man, relax," Jerome said. "I approved it. It's just a couple of jars of sauce and a bit of pasta."

"And what is this?" Regan grabbed the remnants of Parmesan and slammed it back down again on the cheese board.

"That would be Parmesan," Jerome said.

"That would be Parmesan," Regan parroted. "I know what it is. It's something that every resident would give their left eye for right now." He turned to Rylie and stared with such vicious intensity that Rylie thought his eyes might burst into flames.

"Rylie. As governor, how the hell do you think this will look to everyone else?"

"I think it will look like a team celebrating their efforts. Getting to know each other. Supporting one another."

"This is NOT the way to do it." He slammed his palm on the table. Everyone jumped. "I'm sorry, I won't be party to this." Regan pushed his chair backwards, nearly tipping it over. Luke had to grab it to keep it from falling over. "Governor, I'll see you in the morning."

"Come on, man. Don't be like that," Jerome called after him as he stalked out the door and pulled it hard behind him.

"Good riddance," said Kate. "More for us, now."

They sat in awkward silence. The broccoli steamed. The garlicky goodness of the tomato sauce filled the room.

"He's got a point," Imogen said, finally.

"Maybe he does, maybe he doesn't," said Luke. "In any case, I suggest we eat this delicious food now. Otherwise, we might be accused of wasting food as well as taking it."

"That guy," Jerome said, shaking his head. "He just doesn't know how to relax and have fun."

"You're being incredibly nice to him considering how he treats you," Eve said as she took a bite of her pasta.

"He means well. He's got crazy standards is all. I figure he's nursing some big pain in his life."

"Why do you say that?" Luke asked.

"No one is that hard for no reason. I bet his tough skin grew over a giant wound."

"A bloody massive hole to be that much of a dick," Kate muttered.

"Ah, come on. He's got good intentions," Jerome said. He picked a piece of broccoli from the serving platter and bit into it with gusto. "We just need to feed him up and he'll be all right."

Eventually the chatter picked up again as they savoured the meal. The wine flowed and laughter filled the room.

"So. Jerome. What's your deal?" Kate asked with a bit of a slur as she drained her glass and held it up for a refill to Jerome.

"How do you mean?" he said.

"What did you do before Terra Blanca? How did you qualify? Who have you got left on the mainland? That sort of thing." She looked at him with semi-closed eyes, trying to keep him in focus.

Jerome finished pouring, put the bottle down, and leaned back in his chair with a sinewy sensuality that Rylie found hard to ignore.

"I worked in the family business. We have a hydroponic shed just outside of Montreal."

"What did you grow?" Imogen asked.

"Greens, mostly. But I was working on genetic splicing projects. You know – for rapid-growth high-yield crops."

"Why did ya leave?" Kate asked with a belch.

Jerome shrugged. "Wanted my own gig for a while. Plus, Mum needed time to sell the business. Funny, you know. I really miss her. She was a tough boss, but decent. A bit like Regan." He laughed. "She wants to move to Terra Blanca."

"Her and every other man and his dog," Imogen said.

"Well, she's got the skills, so I think she'll make the next round of applications. Who's on that subcommittee, anyway?"

Imogen and Kate raised their hands.

"Sweet! You'll make sure she gets in, eh?" He gave them a winsome smile.

"They'll do no such thing," Rylie said. "Every case on merit, Jerome."

"Sure. I know that. Just asking, is all."

Rylie relaxed over the course of the evening as she watched her colleagues unwind. But the Regan incident was a festering sore at the back of her mind. She tried to ignore it and encouraged everyone to enjoy themselves. Even Luke got a little animated in his banter. *Yes*, she thought, *this was a good idea. An excellent one, in fact. Damn Regan and his sour mood.* She would have to do it again. In a month or so. A surprise for their six months of service. Yes, that would be perfect. And she might not invite Regan next time.

When the meal was done and they were all stuffed to the gills with food, wine, and desserts, Rylie stood at the door and bid them all a good night. She felt a little like royalty thanking her departing guests. Rylie noticed that Imogen lingered behind. She hadn't really settled into the festivities, thought Rylie. Something was troubling her.

"What is it, Imogen?"

"Rylie, I am not sure how this will play out in the community."

"How do you mean?"

"It's not a great look. Us, the council, indulging. Especially when the food supply is so tight right now. Regan and his team are working really hard to get supply up to optimum levels, but we're still short on lots of stuff. People are cranky and grumbling. And here we are, riding high on the hog."

Rylie felt her hackles go up. Some gratitude. "We're not 'riding high'. I hardly call one nice dinner for several months of hard work an excess. Come now, we encourage all teams to take time out and celebrate. How are we any different?"

"We're not. It's just that—"

"Exactly. We're like any other team. We need to press pause from time to time and enjoy our hard work. If we're always focused on the next task, then we run the risk of building resentment on the team. Then what? Burn out. People quitting. We need this first council to get it right. So that others will be willing to take on the role when their time comes."

"But we don't have the whole team here anyway. We're kind of missing one person: Regan. And he didn't exactly support the dinner. And I think there are quite a few others who will have trouble reconciling our dinner as 'fair'."

"Really? How would they see it then?" Rylie crossed her arms and stepped back from Imogen to take her in better. Rylie felt the wine fuel her defiance. She wasn't usually so defensive as a leader. A tingle of caution crept up her spine.

"I think others would see this as a privilege. Unfair. Like we're taking advantage of our position."

"Nonsense. One meal hardly makes us into criminals screwing the system."

"I'm not saying that. I'm just saying that this is what it might look like."

"Okay then. Duly noted. We'll keep this private for the time being."

"Private? I think that's worse. Secrets rarely lead to understanding later."

"Oh, come on, Imogen. I went to all this trouble to show some appreciation for my colleagues and all I get is criticism. I can't win around here."

Imogen flinched at the retort. She considered Rylie for a moment and then said, "I didn't mean to offend. Just sharing my concerns."

Rylie felt her head pound. The rich food had made her queasy. It was late, and she just wanted to get to bed. See if she could sleep off the booze and chocolate cake.

She knew she had lost her cool with Imogen. Regret soured her mood and her stomach a little more. She took a deep breath and tried to still her whirling head.

"Okay. Let's leave it there. I hear your concerns. I'll talk to Regan tomorrow about food production. See if we can get some good news going."

"Thanks."

Rylie touched the younger woman's forearm.

"You're welcome, Imogen. And Imo – thanks for your service."

Imogen gazed at her without saying anything then left.

Leadership sucks, thought Rylie. *Damned if you do, damned if you don't.*

CHAPTER SEVENTEEN

"IN YOU GO, Jerome!" Regan shoved the smaller man into the compost shed.

"You can't lock me up in here, Delarge! That's inhuman!"

"Listen up, Jerome, what's inhuman is your consistent lack of performance. Your consistent slacking off. Your consistent whining. And now I've discovered your dirty little secret: illegal marijuana cropping! What gives you the right to horde this from others? You're a disgrace!"

"Even so, you can't lock me up here! That's against my rights!"

"You will stay here until you complete your work assignment. You're on pest control – you need to scrub and check all the compost bins for unwelcome critters. It's not hard, Jerome. Get it done, then I'll let you out."

"C'mon, man! This is crazy! You can't keep me here!"

Regan closed the door and bolted it shut.

Jerome pounded the door in response.

"C'mon, Delarge! Let me out, you son of a bitch!"

Regan walked away and rubbed his hands in satisfaction. That turd Jerome was finally neutralised. He'd set a real good example for the rest of them. They needed some discipline. And they needed to see that poor performance was not going to happen on his watch.

∽

"You locked him in the compost shed?" Rylie was incredulous. Kate and Imogen were aghast. Even Luke looked shocked.

Regan was nonplussed.

"That dipshit has been nothing but trouble since the beginning. He's slacking big time on the job. That's just not on. It was the quickest way to deal with the situation so he would not influence anyone else."

"Did you have to put him in the compost shed, though? We have isolation protocols for community regulation breaches. He's to be contained in his accommodation."

"I understand that. But I really don't think he would get the lesson if he was locked up in his own room. All the creature comforts and all that. It hardly shows consequences for actions, does it? Think of the example. Tired of working and want a little break? Just break a few rules and you'll be confined to quarters for a while. It's hardly promoting pro-social behaviour."

"And locking someone in a shed is?" Luke Finnegan piped up.

Regan was surprised by Luke's comments. Usually, he was on board with his suggestions. Luke had backed most of his motions and proposals in council so far. He'd thought he had an ally there.

"This is going to make terrific headlines," said Eve. She attended all council meetings in person now, to make sure she got "the right scoop", as she told Rylie.

Regan blanched at Eve's comments. The kid had been vicious in her criticism of the Vertical Farm since he took over. It had become a daily topic of ire amidst the rank and file. What did the brat Addison kid have to say about us today, they grumbled, as headlines ran with tidbits like, "Delarge struggles to deliver" and "Vertical Farm falls short again".

Regan glared at her and continued, "Look, Jerome was just not getting it. No matter how many times I or any of the other crew pulled him up for slacking, or for being selfish, or even just not being a decent human, he just kept on keeping on." Regan looked at the surrounding faces and saw varying degrees of alarm. "This was a good way to show the seriousness of his action. To shock him into awareness. Shake him up a little. Big fella – Vincent – what would you have done?"

The Dopplebot swivelled to face Regan.

"Jerome Gagnon is a conniving scoundrel. He should do his job. The compost shed is his workplace. It's reasonable to keep him there to finish the work. If he can't do his job, sack his ass."

Regan grinned in triumph. Sometimes that big bag of wire and putty hit the right spot.

"That's a little harsh," Rylie said.

"Thank you for the feedback. If he can't do his job, change his job."

Rylie ignored the Dopplebot. "Regan, you can't just go around throwing people into sheds. It's uncivilised."

"And Jerome's behaviour is? Civilised?"

"Even so, you can't just treat him like an animal, Regan. Punishment has not really been shown to rectify behaviour."

Luke again. That twat, thought Regan.

"Punishment is exactly what he deserves, for acting like an animal."

"That's enough, Regan. You will release him immediately and confine him to quarters, as per the protocol. We will meet in a special council to determine the next steps in this incident. For Jerome. And for you, Regan."

"What – for *me*? If you want to talk about protocols, the protocol in this case is clear, Governor. I have jurisdiction over the Vertical Farm, including the management of its workers. I have breached no rules in confining Jerome to the compost shed. He has duties there to keep him occupied and is under no duress. It's called putting a foot down and setting standards. We've all got a role to play. He's not doing his, so I'm doing mine."

"I think you're overlooking something, Regan." Heads swivelled to the voice in the corner. Imogen Bussle.

What's she got to say now? Regan wondered. The woman was never short of opinions.

"Oh yeah? What's that?" Regan said with just a hint of menace.

"You're not going to win any favours with the rest of the crew if they know you go around locking people up. If you lead with threats, you'll reap only fear. Cornered animals tend to fight pretty hard for their freedom. Sometimes to the death." Her eyes held his with an iron he hadn't seen before.

"Oh, really?" Regan felt the flush of anger through his body. His chest expanded and his face reddened. "Well, I can tell you that in my thirty years of leading teams, of running businesses, that a strong arm keeps people in line. People respect strength. They love it. It makes them feel safe. People want to know there is someone there who will maintain standards. Who won't put up with bullshit."

"I'm pretty sure that locking people up doesn't make them feel safe."

Luke again. *What the hell is his problem today?*

"I disagree, Finnegan. I invite all the council to come on down and visit the Farm. It's about bloody time you ventured out of this pampered padded cell and had a look at where the real work is happening. Where people are working hard to feed everyone – including you lot. Come and talk to the people there. And the dock workers. Ask them about my leadership, and if they like their jobs working under me."

"*Under* you? Since when is this a dictatorship? We're a collective, Regan!" Imogen got to her feet and approached Regan. She moved like a hunting fox, all stealth and grace.

Imogen's cool demeanour rattled him. He was used to people backing off when he dialled up the energy. Regan scrambled to contain his impulses.

"You know what I mean," he replied.

"I am not sure that I do. Locking up Jerome doesn't look like the actions of a reasonable leader," she continued.

"All right, enough." Rylie stepped between them. "We will settle this with council process. To be reconvened

tomorrow morning. After a visit to the Farm. And Regan—
" She pointed up at the big man. "You will release Jerome immediately and confine him to his quarters pending our investigation of this matter. Is that understood?"

Regan's pulse thundered in his temple. His nostrils flared and he sucked in a deep breath to restrain what wanted to fly from his mouth. He nodded instead and glared at each of them in turn. *We're not done yet*, he thought and stomped off.

CHAPTER EIGHTEEN

What game was Regan playing? wondered Luke. Locking up Jerome was a dumb move. It would only undermine his own position, not rankle the council. If Regan was also an agent, then he'd made an unforced error. There was no way the council would support Regan in locking people up. This was a punishment approach. From the outset the community had adhered to a "no punishment" philosophy. Consequences, yes. Atonement, yes. Rehabilitation, yes. Restorative justice, yes.

Punishment?

No. Too basic and rudimentary for a sophisticated and small community like this. Regan would know all that. Did he hope to undermine this system as part of testing the overall Terra Blanca ideology? That might be it. But hadn't people moved on from militant crime and punishment leadership?

What was Regan trying to accomplish? This just didn't

make sense. Luke decided he was going to have to find out for himself.

He started with Shane.

"Shane!" The small, quiet man looked up from the lettuces he was tending in the shed and turned back to his work.

"What do you want?"

"Hey, relax. I'm here to be supportive."

"Oh, yeah? Just like last time? Real supportive. Didn't stop Miss Evie Addison having a real swipe."

"I know. I know. It was a crappy article."

"You said that right." Shane plucked a slug from the lettuce and chucked it in a bucket to be added to the insect protein slush.

"Anyway, I'm here on council business. I'm investigating the incident with Jerome."

Shane sniffed and scowled. "What do you want to know?"

"How's it going down here? With Regan? With Jerome?"

"Jerome? The guy is a slack-ass. A smooth talker who skives off from everything. He deserved everything he got."

"I see." Luke reached in and checked a couple of lettuces alongside Shane. He found another slug, dropped it in the bucket, and watched it squirm.

"And working with Regan? What's that like?"

"Regan? He's tough. But a hard worker. No one works harder than Regan."

"Is he a good boss?"

Shane paused and stretched his back.

"He's a decent enough boss. He's a hard task master, that's for sure. He's harsh. But fair."

"What do you like about working with him?"

Shane wiped his fingers down his sopping shirt, looked around for his water bottle and then took a big swig.

"What I like about Regan Delarge is that he speaks his mind. He's not afraid to speak the truth. He says it how it is. He's a real strong leader. Hard-nosed. But he's one of the guys. I really like that about him. Makes you feel like you're part of something."

"And do the women feel the same?"

Shane took another gulp of water, placed the bottle on the ground and resumed his slug hunt.

"Can't say I would know how the women feel. I'm down here a lot on my own. Not enough people to go around, you see."

"I do see. And I know how hard it is." Luke clapped Shane on the back. "Thanks, Shane. I appreciate your time. And I appreciate all the work you do."

Shane nodded and continued his grim slug-hunting.

Luke made his way to the staff lunchroom. He interrupted a group of four young workers who were just finishing their lunch.

"Ten – shun! Councillor on deck!" one of them said.

"At ease, gentlemen." Luke played along. "Finish your lunch. And if you don't mind, I've a got a few questions for you as you do." Luke noticed two women were at another table in the corner, sitting hunched over and talking in whispers. He nodded at them.

"So," Luke said, and smiled at the foursome. "Tell me what you think about working here. Your boss Regan, for instance."

They glanced at each other. One of them leaned back in his chair, his pimple-ridden chin bobbing at Luke.

"Regan is awesome! He doesn't take shit from anybody, and he runs a tight ship. He works his tail off and expects the same of us."

Luke nodded and turned to the next man.

"I got no complaints. I count myself lucky to be here."

"Same."

"Me too."

"And what do you think of the incident with Jerome? You agree with him getting locked up?"

They chortled.

"He had it coming to him. Always making excuses, that one. He has his head more often between someone's legs than in the cabbages." More snickering.

"I see. Well, thanks so much. Don't let me hold you from your work."

"No problem. Any time you want to see the real workers, you come right on down and join us, Councillor."

Luke watched them go, their strides filled with the swagger of male youth. Then he turned to the two remaining workers who were sweeping up the crumbs of their sandwiches.

"Excuse me, before you go, may I ask you a few questions, too?" Luke asked.

They exchanged glances and gestured for him to sit.

"What's it like for you working here?"

There was an awkward pause. The older woman leaned forward. Luke saw that her dark hair was pulled back so tightly into a pony tail that it tugged at the skin of her forehead. The flesh around her eyes sagged in folds and the pungent scent of days-old sweat leaked from her shirt as she shifted in her chair.

"We don't want any trouble," she said in a low voice.

"Of course not."

"That Regan Delarge is a dog. He's a real bully. He's always yelling, shouting people down, telling them they're no good."

"And he's sexist." The younger worker straightened her shirt, tugging it by its front so that the wrinkles flattened. Luke watched the bulk of her tongue work its way around her gums, seeking lunch crumbs.

"Oh?"

"Sure is," the younger woman continued. "It's always about 'the guys', 'the boys', 'the men'. He tolerates the women because he needs us to do the work, but he's not at all interested in us. He's never even asked me my name. Sherrene, by the way." She held out her hand, then remembered to brush the lunch remnants stuck to her fingers on her shirt before extending it again.

"Luke."

"Cecily."

"So, Cecily, Sherrene, what did you think about the incident with Jerome?"

They glanced at each other again and then Cecily leaned forward and spoke in whispers.

"Look, Jerome is a skirt-chaser and an outrageous flirt. He wasn't the best manager. But since his demotion he gets on with it. He does his work." She tapped the table with her forefinger.

Sherrene leaned forward too, making sure no one was watching or listening to them.

"Plus, he's the only one game enough to stand up to Regan. So Regan has it in for him. Classic bullying."

"I see. Anything else?"

"Look, it's tough down here. The work is physical and there is not a lot of joy in it. But Regan? He just makes it worse. At least with Jerome we had a bit of fun."

"Well, then. Thanks for your time. I appreciate your candour."

Luke returned to his accommodation and pondered this for a while. How would the governor handle trouble in the workforce? Was this something that could be resolved through the workers? Was Regan trying to create divisions in the labour on purpose? Was this the angle Regan was using to test the Terra Blanca systems? A type of socialist schism? Or was he trying to do a throwback to old ways of command-and-control as part of the challenge?

Luke didn't like it. It was unsettling. What was even more strange for him, was that he felt disturbed by this. He had gone into this assignment with curiosity about whether the Terra Blanca system could withstand challenges around the edges. But he discovered he didn't like where Regan was taking the test. Luke realised that he wanted Terra Blanca to be successful and he was surprised to discover he actually cared about it. He didn't want to see the whole thing go up in flames.

Furthermore, he had come to admire Rylie as a leader. She was gracious and compassionate. She gave everyone a chance, and she treated all issues with fair consideration. Luke had little tingles of regret about how his subtle undermining was affecting her leadership. But that was the whole point of this, wasn't it? He was deliberately poking at the edges to find a sore spot so that these could be made stronger in the future. His subterfuge was in service to a greater end.

But still, Luke felt a little guilty. Something was not quite sitting right. Maybe it was the conflict that was growing in the Vertical Farm. He'd better keep a very close eye on this.

CHAPTER NINETEEN

"Fuck a duck!" Regan swore as Marty gave him the Vertical Farm production report. Output was still down. People had been complaining about the quality of the zucchinis and lettuce. The fruit trees had some strange blight on them, and everything was wilting because the cooling system was on the blitz.

"We need more people on this. Can we assign extra crews?"

"We've already got people on overtime. They're not happy about it."

"I don't give a rat's ass about their happiness. We've got to get this food production system fixed pronto. If we don't, let them explain to their neighbours that we're all starving because they weren't 'happy' about doing a bit of extra work."

"Even so, they're not really cooperating."

"Oh, yeah? Who? Who is not cooperating?"

"Jerome. And a few others."

"Jerome! That little shit. I knew I should have made an example of him! Rylie, that meddling, soft-headed do-gooder. She ruined the discipline I was just getting established here." Regan fumed for a moment.

"Marty, call an all-hands. It's time to put a rocket up a few backsides!"

❧

The Vertical Farm teams gathered in the main atrium amidst the tomato vines. The mood was sombre. They had been working long hours and knew the community depended on them. Like their neighbours', their dinner plates were meagre. So far, they had failed to live up to expectations.

"Listen up!" Regan boomed. "I'm not going to sug-ar-coat this. Our production is below subsistence and some of our crops are at risk of failure. I need you all to step up and put in some extra effort. If we all pitch in, we can get some of the sheds that are behind production kicked into overdrive, and then we can get things back to where they should be. If we all do our bit, we'll do fine."

"You can't keep driving us like slaves!"

Jerome. That dickwad, thought Regan.

"We're all working twelve-hour days already!" added someone else.

Regan listened to a few other voices protest while his frustration gathered steam.

"What did you think, coming to Terra Blanca? That this was a free ride? You all got lottery tickets, same as me. We're lucky to get a break. A place to live that's pretty decent, compared to the cramped and stinking places on the mainland. But it needs work. A lot of work to get it up and running properly." He puffed his chest and stood tall, letting his bulk amplify his message.

"Now, we're in charge of the food. That's the most important role on the island. We screw this up, and we all suffer. We all go hungry. And that means we need to step up and do what it takes. Longer hours if needs be to get the work done. If that means fourteen hours or sixteen hours, that is what we'll do. So that we can be proud that we can feed ourselves and our neighbours. Now, who is too precious to do a few hours of extra labour? Who is freeloading off the rest of us?" Regan's square jaw set like a cement brick and his eyes narrowed with a blazing fury.

"I get that we're under pressure. You just can't keep driving us to exhaustion. We have labour laws to follow."

Jerome again.

Regan's eyes fixed on Jerome with a burning intensity.

"Anyone feel the way Jerome does?"

There was an awkward shuffling and then a handful of hands went up.

"Good. Good." Regan's face was flushed. But his voice stayed calm.

"You're excused from work. On one condition. You explain to the rest of Terra Blanca how you're freeloading on the hard work of your neighbours. Why you have a day off while they toil for the greater good."

"C'mon, man…" Jerome looked dejected. "It's not about having a day off. It's about being reasonable."

"Reasonable!" boomed Regan. "You try telling the hungry people of Terra Blanca what's reasonable when they go to bed with rumbling stomachs. Try telling them that you couldn't be bothered to work a few extra shifts to get the food production sorted. That this was a 'reasonable' choice to make."

"Regan, c'mon!" Jerome persisted. "We've got other solutions we can play with. We can get the bots re-programmed. We can borrow people from other areas…"

"Been there, done that! Look, Jerome. I'm in charge here. I've got responsibility for the outcomes of this farm, and for how we get there. And that means a bit of hard work now so we can reap the rewards later. I'm proud of this crew. We can get this done. We just won't tolerate people dragging the chain around us." Regan glanced around him. Some were sour-faced. Most were open, if a little fatigued.

"Who wants to get this place pumping? Who wants to make us proud? Who's with me?" Regan bellowed.

A chorus of approval greeted him.

Jerome shook his head. Regan could see him grumble to someone next to him.

"If you don't like it, you're welcome to leave. And tell everyone else why you abandoned your post and left it to others to take up the slack." Regan pushed his way through the crowd to stand looming over Jerome.

"What do you choose, Jerome?"

Jerome scowled at him. He shrugged and moved away.

"That's what I thought. You've come to your senses. Now, let's get this operation rebooted. Marty has the new plan."

Regan stood back and watched with a scorching gaze as Marty outlined the new roster and production plan. Some glanced over at him and nodded. Others avoided him.

Regan felt a burn of satisfaction. Things were finally getting under control.

CHAPTER TWENTY

"GOVERNOR, I'D LIKE to move a motion of objection against Regan Delarge." Luke stood to make his point. The other councillors stared at him.

"What is the nature of the objection, Luke?" Rylie asked.

"Abusive and coercive behaviour towards the teams at the Docks and the Vertical Farm. I have testimonies from numerous people about his aggressive style. I have a petition of some ninety-seven names who have signed on as objectors. He needs to be removed as leader immediately."

"Like hell." Regan Delarge leaned over the Nest's oak table. His voice was low and brooding, a cloud growing heavy and dark. "Finnegan, you're a no-good meddler. Things are working just fine down there."

"Regan, this is serious business," Rylie said.

"It's MY business, Governor." He poked his giant

finger into the table. "Especially if some troublemaker is undermining my authority."

"Your authority in the Vertical Farm is temporarily delegated by the council, Regan," Rylie said with a cautioning tone.

"And I've been doing a fine job, thanks very much."

"Not according to the majority of your workforce," Luke said.

"You've been stirring them up, Finnegan. Things were going along just fine before you showed up."

"I think you'll find that the objectors have long had issues before I stepped in."

"The objectors? What is that? A secret society?"

"The objectors are concerned workers and citizens. They've all signed and registered their complaints."

"Oh, yeah? Tell me who." Regan glared at Luke.

"You can read the full list right here." Luke gestured to the screen.

"That's enough." Rylie jumped to her feet. "This is not normal council process. We will hear Luke and the objectors' petition and evaluate it accordingly. And we will refrain from name-calling and intimidation." Rylie stared pointedly at Regan. "Regan, as this concerns you, we will invite your perspective once we have heard from Luke."

"Too right I'm going to stay and listen. I don't trust this sneaky bastard." He narrowed his gaze at Luke and shifted his bulk on the bench.

"Let's proceed," Rylie said.

The presentation continued with Luke itemising numerous issues from the most egregious to the most trivial. The chief complaint was the treatment of Jerome, who many felt was being unfairly singled out. Other issues were clearly personal grudges twisted to slander Regan's leadership, including a complaint about Regan hogging the best coffee mug.

As the issues were read out, Regan's face was puce; he bounced his foot and breathed loudly as he attempted to rein in his outrage. By the time they had run through the huge list, his resolve had boiled to hard, bitter contempt, like soup boiling dry to a foul, smoking crust. When Rylie invited him to speak, his voice was thick with restrained anger.

"That's a long list of issues." He wrestled for his next words. "As you know, I'm a man of action. I'm committed to Terra Blanca and want to make sure we're all fed." His foot bounced, and he rubbed his thighs as he reached for the right words. "I can see how some of my decisions might be seen as… heavy-handed. But I'm determined to make this work." He stopped and tried to let his rage ebb.

"Are you willing to undergo the problem resolution process?" Rylie asked.

Regan's lips flattened into a thin line. He nodded.

"All right, let's begin with the first issue."

Luke sat back, a little deflated. He had hoped that this would be a unanimous, quick execution.

One by one they addressed the complaints. Regan promised to do everything from be more consultative, express a series of public apologies, and give up his claims to the coffee mug. By the end of it he might as well have offered up his left nut on a platter with a "please, ma'am, have another."

Luke was amazed. They walked through every single

issue and somehow Regan came out, if not quite unscathed, still in charge at the Vertical Farm. The council process was designed to allow every problem to be addressed until resolved and accepted by all parties. But how much was Delarge nodding and saying "yes" just to hang onto his job? Would he truly transform his leadership? The proof of the pudding is in the eating, so they say.

CHAPTER TWENTY-ONE

THOSE ARROGANT MOTHERFUCKERS! thought Regan as he dragged himself back to the Vertical Farm. He was going to have to eat a huge piece of humble pie. With a side order of shite. Well, he could play that game. He could play conciliatory. He could even suck up to that limp-dick prat, Jerome. Though it might set his back teeth grinding.

A month passed and Regan made a show of publicly apologising for his behaviour. He admitted he was a tad over-zealous when it came to delivering on results and asked for people's forgiveness. He even promoted Jerome to a crew manager position. Regan astonished himself at how much he could put on a fake smile for that poxy toad.

Some of the workers remained wary. Mostly the ones who had signed the petition and lodged complaints, the so-called 'objectors', Regan noticed. *Too right you'd better be wary*, he thought. *I'll be coming for you at some point.* Once he got the ship back on an even keel, he'd deal with those petty trouble-makers.

Inside, he seethed. He railed against bureaucracy and the council's failure to back him and his work ethic. As he had foreseen, with the reduced work hours, food production was perilously low again. Grumbles had turned away from his leadership and back to food shortages. People were hungry and fed up. Regan bit his tongue and said, with only a tiny hint of sarcasm, "As long as people are being treated well then that is the main thing."

To help alleviate his frustration, Regan spent more time on marine patrol. That's when he and Marty made the discovery…

✺

Peeking out from under one of the docks of the accommodation platform, he caught a glimpse of something blue bobbing in the water.

"Marty, take the boat in closer." Regan leaned over the edge of the patrol unit. He reached out with a grappling hook and tugged at the object. It remained snug, eluding his hook.

"What is it?" Marty called from the helm.

"I think it's a barrel. I can't get it with the hook. If you pull up to the dock, I'll jump in and take a look."

Regan stripped down to his jocks and slipped into the water with a sharp inhale of breath. The icy water stung and he breathed quickly to adjust his core temperature. It always surprised him how cold the water could get in Quebec. Even if it stayed hot outside, like it did most of the year now.

Regan pulled himself under the dock as Marty secured the boat. There wasn't much headroom, so Regan took a breath and dove under to take a look. It was not just one barrel, but several, tied together like a flotilla. He came back up for air.

"Marty, hand me one of the gutting knives, would you? It's barrels, all right. I'll need to cut them free." Regan took the knife from Marty and dove under again. He made quick work of slashing the barrels' mooring and guided them to the surface where Marty hauled them into the boat. There were five in total.

"Shall we take a look?" Marty asked.

"You bet. Nothing usual about this situation."

They released the seal on one of the barrels and lifted the lid. Regan reached in and hauled out the first item. Bread. Marty grabbed the next item, wrapped in paper. He ripped it open. Something perishable in a plastic bag. He opened it up and took a whiff.

"Meat. Pepperoni, I think." Marty took another whiff. "Man, that smells good." He wrapped it up again and peered into the barrel. There was a lot more food in there. Mostly perishables. The cold water must have been keeping it from spoiling.

Regan was dumbfounded. This was a clear breach of Terra Blanca import bans. Someone was smuggling. Either for personal supply, or for black market trade.

"Well, shit," he said at last. "Let's take this back to the depot and unpack it carefully. We don't want any bio-security breaches. Plus, we need to document the find. What dock number is this?"

"Twelve."

"All right. We'll start our investigation with the residents who access this dock."

"What are we going to do with the food? Once we've audited it?"

"We'll keep it secure in the supply reserves."

"We won't destroy it, will we?" Marty's face looked pained.

Regan shrugged. "That will be for council to decide."

"That would be a shame. We're all starving."

"Who should get it, though?"

"Some lucky bastard."

"Really? You'd be happy for someone to get it?"

"Better than throwing it out."

"I don't know. Hungry people don't do well watching their neighbour get more than their fair share."

"I suppose you're right." Marty took another glance in the barrel. "There's cheese in here, Regan." Then he shook his head and sealed it up again.

"If some get, we should all get."

"One block of cheese won't go around three hundred people, Regan. Maybe we should run a lottery or something."

"Maybe. Or maybe a competition for the hardest working."

"Oh yeah? And who would judge that?"

"The hardest worker, of course. Me."

"You're nuts, Regan. You pick the winner of this haul based on how hard you think they're working, and you'll cause a riot. Half the Vertical Farm have it in for you already."

"Maybe. But it might make them work a little harder

if they knew they'd get dibs on stuff like this." Regan dried himself off with a towel stashed at the front of the boat and then pulled his clothes back on.

"Anyway, this is all academic for now. Let's get this stuff counted and safe, then the council can figure out what's next."

∽

Rylie and the councillors considered the list of goods confiscated by Regan. It was the biggest find yet. Too much food for a single household to consume. The culprits must either share between households or run it as a black-market operation. Neither option was good.

"Clearly, we have a serious situation here," Imogen said. "One or more Terra Blancans are wilfully breaching their citizenship agreements and putting the community at risk."

"It's a pretty low risk from a bio-security point of view," Jerome said. He scratched his chest then flicked through the images on the council displays. "Bread. Cheese. Crackers. Some dried meats. No fruit or vegetables. We've tested it all. Nothing that will infest our own production."

"That's not the point, Jerome." Regan restrained himself before calling him an idiot. "Even if there was nothing in this lot, what else might get set loose if they continue? Plus, this is a threat to security. We need to know absolutely everything and everyone coming in and out of this island if we are going to survive. Especially given the food production situation as it is now."

"We also need to sort out what we'll do with those perishables." Kate leaned over the table to steer the conversation away from the bulls butting heads. "I'd be happy to dispose of the goods. I haven't had pepperoni in a good long while."

"None of us are getting the contraband," Rylie said with a hint of exasperation. "This is clearly a large-scale community issue. The smuggling is a symptom of our food production system not up to scratch. If things were working according to plan, residents would have all these niceties and we'd be dealing with some other issue. But for now, we've got hungry people, and some that are trying to either circumvent that or profit from it. Our best solution is to get food working." Rylie drummed her fingers on the table. "I suggest we shut down work on the new accommodation platform, and the Innovation Centre, and put all hands on deck. Jerome, if we reinstate you at the Vertical Farm as Manager, we can get Regan to focus on aquaculture. We could use the marine patrol boats to help with harvest. If we get more seafood on people's plates that might keep a bit of hunger at bay."

Regan opened his mouth to say something, then shut it again. He'd just been sidelined from the Farm, but he'd been given aquaculture. A decent trade. He wouldn't mind a break from the surliness of the Vertical Farm crew anyhow.

"Good," he added slowly. "I'll be able to focus on uncovering the smuggling operation." He ran his hand over the edge of the oak table, feeling the shapes of the owls etched there. "I also propose we have a lockdown on visits. No one off the island. Just until we sort this out."

"Whoa. That's a bit drastic, isn't it?" Luke said. He'd been quiet through the discussion. His brows furrowed together, thinking through the ramifications. "Not sure people will like being shut down like that."

"Well, the *people* ought to have thought about that before they started breaking all the rules and putting us all at risk." Regan's voice had a streak of ice.

"Still…"

"Regan's in charge of security so we will follow his advice on this one," Rylie interjected. "Off-island visits are banned until we resolve the smuggling."

"What should we do about the contraband?" Kate tried again.

"Let's put it to the community. They can choose."

The community chose a lottery. Five households won a portion of the contraband. And they shared with their neighbours. While most missed out, they were happy they'd had a say in the distribution of the largesse.

The joy was short-lived. Regan started his systematic searching of each accommodation shortly after that. He'd find the traitor come hell or high water.

Except that he didn't. No place was spared. And no more contraband was found.

"Damn it," he said as he left the final home with Marty in tow.

A young woman who worked at the aquaculture processing shed slammed the door behind him.

"You're welcome!" she spat through the closed door.

Now what, he wondered. It had taken him and the marine patrol crew three weeks to get through all the properties. Their boats were busy during the day to help with kelp and mollusc harvest, so they'd had to do the searches in the evening. His team was exhausted.

All the teams were sapped. Food production shifts had been extended to twelve hours while rationing had been introduced. People were hungry and tired.

Regan and Marty travelled back along the shore path towards their own accommodation in silence.

"Hey."

Regan looked up, startled. It was Luke.

"Finnegan! What are you doing out here?"

"Looking for you. We've got a problem."

"What now?"

"The Vertical Farm teams are on strike."

"What?"

"They're on strike. They're refusing to do anymore work."

"What the hell? Why?"

"They're protesting the security measures, the long shifts, the restrictions."

Regan took a moment to compose himself. Marty looked shocked.

"You want us to break it up? Send them home?"

"No. Not at all. Rylie is calling for all councillors to come and meet them in the Vertical Farm. We've got to negotiate."

"Negotiate? They're stopping food production and they want to negotiate? They ought to be shot for treason."

"Come now, that's a little extreme. They're tired and hungry. That's all. I'm sure we can smooth this over." Luke reached out and patted the big man's shoulder. It was hard and ropy.

The three of them hurried to the Vertical Farm. Rylie and the other councillors were inside with the night shift crew. Jerome was doing placating gestures to the crowd as Rylie tried to speak.

"Hold on. Let the governor have her say. You too, Sarah. I've got my eye on you." Jerome pointed two fingers at his eyes, then pointed them at a handsome middle-aged woman with red hair near the front. He winked at her and gave her a lopsided smile. She blushed.

"Thanks, Jerome. Listen, here's what I'm hearing. You're tired. You're overworked. You're hungry. I get that. We can do something about that. I've discussed it with Jerome, and we will open up the reserves and supplement every Terra Blancan household with extras for a week or so. The meat lab is nearly production-ready and—"

"Finally!" someone yelled out.

"—we'll increase seafood portions, too. There is nothing we can do about the vegetable harvest, as you know. You've done an outstanding job getting it in full production, but those damn plants just don't grow any faster. As for security, I'll hand you over to Regan." Rylie glanced at Regan and nodded. "Can you give us an update?"

"Thanks, Governor. Our initial investigation is complete. Thank you for letting us into your homes."

"As if we had a choice," murmured someone.

Regan ignored that and continued. "We have yet to find the smugglers. If that person or persons were to come forward, then we could apprehend them and—"

"If I may," Rylie interrupted. "The council's position is that whoever was responsible for the barrels was motivated by hunger. We get it. It's been tough. We're behind our supply schedule. But we're nearly back on track and there will be no need for secret supplies. So, if someone comes forward, no harm done. We can move on and lift the off-island visit ban."

That undermining bitch, Regan thought. Security was his purview and she had just made a decree without discussing it with him. Or the rest of the council, for that matter.

No one spoke up. Regan scrutinised each face, looking for signs of guilt. Someone knew something, damn them.

Rylie let the silence stretch into discomfort. Still, no one spoke up. There was an awkward cough and blank looks.

"You may come and see me privately. Once we know who is responsible, we will lift the off-island ban. In the meantime, Jerome will open the reserve store tomorrow morning and distribute supplemental packs to each household. Thank you."

Rylie turned and walked past Regan with a glance. He glared back at her.

"What were you going to do when you 'apprehended' someone?" Luke asked Regan as the room dissolved into murmurs and movement. "Lock them in the compost shed again?" He bumped shoulders with Regan in jest.

"It would be more than they deserved."

And with that, he walked away.

CHAPTER TWENTY-TWO

OFF-ISLAND VISIT BAN:
A SECURITY ISSUE OR HUMAN
RIGHTS VIOLATION?

RYLIE DELETED THE news story in annoyance. It had been a week since the strike and the amnesty offer, but still no one had come forward. They'd have to relent soon. Eve was right in her article. This was too much. They couldn't isolate people indefinitely. It had been a month already. They didn't need more unrest. At least the food situation had somewhat abated. Rylie stood and walked over to the council window overlooking the green space of Terra Blanca's central platform. The wind bent the trees in a vigorous dance. Rain spat at the window.

"Rylie, we've got a situation." Regan pushed himself through the doorway, his face red from exertion.

"Yes, I've read the article."

"What?"

"Eve's article. We'll have to lift the ban."

"Ah – no – not that. I mean, yes, probably. But that's not the problem. We've got a storm situation. We've picked up a major storm cell heading our way. It's massive. We need to go into lockdown."

"Really? Show me." She thrust the tablet at him, and he pulled up the weather chart and alarm system.

"Oh my God. How bad is it?"

"Category four. Maybe five."

"How long have we got?"

"Maybe twelve hours."

"Will the platform anchors hold up to it?"

"That's what they've been designed for. But this will be the first big test."

"All right. You sound the storm warning and make the announcement. I'll alert the councillors for an emergency session in the Nest."

"Roger that. I'll be there in ten."

Rylie didn't wait. She punched in a summons to the councillors, then grabbed her jacket and paused as she looked again out the window. Gulls squawked and beat furiously against a headwind. The trees whipped backwards and forward in athletic devotion to an angry sky.

She, too, said a prayer to the weather gods.

The Terra Blancans gathered in the Nest. As the central floating platform, it was the most stable. It also had a kitchen and its own emergency reserves in case of damage to the supply platform.

People made themselves as comfortable as possible, having brought pillows and bedding, anticipating a long night. With people and their belongings everywhere in the stands, Rylie and the councillors set up the storm response war room in one of the offices on the outer ring of the Nest. They had a view of the citizens in the arena while they could also track the storm's progress on several display monitors that Imogen and her crew had brought over from the Innovation Centre.

They stood before the screens, jittery. Kate chewed her fingernails. Imogen flicked from screen to screen, tracking the path of the storm. Jerome coughed and rubbed his head as if to clear the stress. Regan had his arms crossed, staring down the info as it flashed across the display. Vincent was positioned in a corner, ready to be called upon if needed.

Rylie felt Luke watching her. She knew she was grim-faced but resolved. Not panicky. Yet. She tried to feel confident she'd stay the course and get them through. Provided Terra Blanca held together and kept its moorings.

The wind came screeching like an enraged raptor, hurling itself against the Nest. Walls shook. Windows rattled. Residents cowered. Shrieks pierced their courage.

The rain came. Spitting and hissing.

"Whoa! The Nest is moving!" Jerome spread his arms wide to maintain balance as the floor seemed to ripple. The hexagonal shape of the modular platforms helped dissipate the wave energy, but even so, the storm wreaked havoc.

There was the sound of smashing glass and a gush of wind.

"Where is that?" Kate demanded. "Where is that damage, Imo? What do the sensors say?"

"Outer ring. One of the office windows overlooking the central plaza." She flicked the screen to that room. Chairs were flung back against the far wall as the ravenous wind and rain licked the corners of the room.

"Too dangerous to seal it up. We'll have to wait. Bring up the camera for the Nest roof, Imo, please." Kate chewed on her thumbnail.

The Nest roof was a concern. Though the glass was reinforced, and nothing hung over it, this wind tossed loose shoes, plants, and other stray objects like shot-puts. They all worried the roof would crash under the barrage.

Rylie gripped Luke's arm. She yelled into his ear to be heard over the storm. "Go tell them to move to the sides of the arena, away from the roof!"

The rain turned to hail and bombarded the building. Luke looked at her, puzzled, and she yelled again, enunciating each word. She gestured to the arena and made a parting motion.

At last he understood, gave a thumbs-up and rushed away.

The sky darkened and the lights flickered. There was a flash and a giant crack of thunder. They shrieked and cowered.

"Look at the water!" Jerome yelled and pointed at the shoreline display. The waves were black and frothing with white spume. They rolled in giant crests towards them.

"What about the boats?" Regan bawled.

Imogen flicked to the border control dock. The boats cavorted with the waves, straining at their tethers.

"I hope you were good with the knots!" Kate cried.

Regan stared back and squashed his lips together in stern response.

Eve burst into the room after Luke. Her face was ashen and her clothes soaked.

"Mum!" she wailed and rushed into Rylie's arms. Another enormous flash and roaring boom. Rylie covered her daughter's head and yelled, "Get down!"

The floor seemed to heave again. The lights faded and then went out.

"Everyone – under the table!" Rylie roared as she guided Eve beside her.

Kate rummaged in her pocket and brought out a light. She crawled under the table with the rest of them.

"I won't be able to go and fix anything until the wind eases a bit," Kate yelled. "The backup power may kick in, but a connection must be busted somewhere. Maybe a lightning strike."

Rylie felt her daughter tremble. She guessed it was partly the shock of the storm's brutality, and partly due to her wet clothes. She rubbed her daughter's back and Eve leaned into her in response. Rylie savoured the tender moment. Eve had been so prickly with her ever since they left the mainland. It was nice to feel needed again.

Imogen squished in beside Eve. Luke and Jerome bent their limbs at awkward angles to shelter under the table, while Regan leaned against the table leg with his legs sprawled out into the room. Kate took up position opposite him, holding her light so it created a central lamp for them all.

The storm rolled and roared, a vulture with screeching talons raking against their puny shelter. Rylie felt humbled and insignificant. She touched her owl necklace for comfort, seeking strength. All they could do was wait.

Thunder exploded. They jerked in fear. Nervous laughter. They marvelled together at the cacophony of the rain and hail. When Jerome grabbed the light from Kate and made scary faces, they giggled. Even Regan rolled his eyes and smiled.

And for the first time, Rylie felt the strands of connection like a sticky frail web between them.

After what felt like hours, there was an easing. The thunder rumbled, distant. They counted the seconds between lightning and the crack. Six seconds…Seven seconds…It was moving away from them, though the wind still howled, and the rain still swooshed and spat.

"I'll go now and check the transformer box," Kate said as she pushed up on her feet, teetering. She pulled her shirt down over her waist as it had crept up while she was hunched under the table. "See if we can get the power back up."

"I can go with you, if you like," Jerome said. "I need to get out of here and stretch my legs. Getting the heebies in here."

"Regan, want to help me with that window that got smashed?" Luke suggested as he moved out from under the table and unfolded his legs. "There might be some plastic bags in the kitchen we can use to seal it off temporarily."

"I'd prefer to check the boats. We're screwed if those come loose."

"Luke, can you check the people in the Nest first, please?" Rylie said. "Make sure everyone's okay before we start on the building."

"I'll go with Luke, Mum," Eve said.

"Are you sure, sweetie?"

"Yes, I'm fine now. I can help in the Nest more than I can here."

"All right. If everyone can return as soon as possible. Once Kate gets the power back up, we will need to assess the damage and make a plan. Imogen, stay here and work with Vincent. See if we can troubleshoot anything with our remote sensors."

"Roger that, boss."

Rylie found her tablet and activated it to see if any of the sensor displays were still reading. Nothing.

"Vincent, can you get me anything on the comms system? Is it still working?" Imogen said.

"My connection to the sensors indicates no damage to communication. The power shortage seems to be isolated to the central platform. No signal from greenhouse number two."

"What? No signal? Is it damaged?"

"That would be the best deduction, Governor."

"Crap. But power is on everywhere else?"

"Yes."

"Right. So power is out on the central hub. Nowhere else. That's good news. Hopefully Kate can have it repaired quickly."

As if in answer, the lights switched back on. There was a cheer from the people in the Nest.

"Good. Now let's get these displays up again."

The screens lit up. The storm still belted the island. Imogen brought up the radar.

"We're on the tail end of it now," she said. "The worst is over."

"Thank goodness for that."

"Vincent, can you draw up list of repair priorities in conjunction with Athena?" Rylie said.

"What on earth is he doing?' Imogen said.

Rylie glanced up at the perimeter camera display. Regan was on one of the docks, putting on a lifejacket. He struggled to stay upright as the wind pounded him.

"He's going after that boat," Rylie said in horror. One of the island border patrol boats drifted away from the dock. Imogen and Rylie watched Regan run and jump into the dark, surging water. He was gone.

Then he bobbed to the surface. He was just visible with the bright yellow life-support vest.

"The man is a bloody lunatic," Imogen said.

Rylie raced through the options. There was no one to send after him. Too dangerous. She didn't want to risk anyone else. She could go herself, but she was an average swimmer at best. Rylie felt her brain seize and her gut fill with dread. It was like watching a movie in freeze frames. She was powerless to do anything but watch.

But Regan seemed to be making headway. He drew closer to the bucking craft. He swam up to its side and managed to grab the ladder at the back near the engine. Rylie squinted and Imogen zeroed in on the image as best she could, but they were drifting further away. They could just make out a flash of yellow at the back of the boat.

"He's still with it!" Imogen called out. "I think the big buffoon managed to get himself on board."

Rylie blinked and her heart raced. She could see Regan on the boat, at the helm. It looked like he'd managed to get it started and was riding the waves around to the lee side of the island. He was safe. She breathed again.

"Bring up the perimeter cameras – I think he might pull up on the processing platform."

Imogen swapped the view, but the screens were dark and there was nothing but the driving rain and angry sky.

And then a light bobbed into view.

"There he is. That boofhead did it."

They watched as he brought the boat up to the processing access dock, jumped nimbly to the platform, and lashed the boat securely. Then he dashed back towards the connection bridge to the Nest where the camera feed cut out.

"I feel sick," Rylie said.

"Here. Have some water." Imogen handed her a bottle from the stash they'd brought into the storm hub. Rylie took a big swig and glanced at the time display.

"Where the hell is everybody? I want everyone back here. Safe."

Regan stopped outside the door and shed the lifejacket. He cradled his left arm and winced as he joined them.

"You hurt?" Imogen said.

"Yeah. The boat smacked me around as I pulled myself onto the deck."

"Let me take a look," Rylie said.

"What were you thinking, you nutter? We had no one to come after you! You could have drowned out there. Then who would boss us around?" Imogen had her hands on her hips, looking up at him.

Regan ignored her and pulled a face as Rylie prodded his arm. It was discoloured and swollen.

"That might be broken. We'll get Luke to run a scan when he's back." She rummaged in the first-aid kit they'd brought with them and retrieved a bandage. "Let's put it in a sling in the meantime." Rylie was conscious of the big man's wet clothes as she tied his arm securely. His skin had goosebumps and he shivered. "Where's your bedding?"

"In the corner there."

She wrapped a blanket around his shoulders. She wasn't sure but she thought she caught a hint of something new in the big man's demeanour. What was it? Sheepishness?

Luke, Jerome, and Kate returned, their rainwear sodden.

"Leave those jackets outside," Imogen said. "It already smells like damp dog in here with Regan all saturated from his little bath."

"What happened?" Luke asked as he walked over to look at Regan's strapped arm.

"It's nothing. We can deal with it later." Regan moved away from Luke's inspection.

"Regan decided he'd play the hero and swim after a boat that floated away," Imogen said.

"You went swimming – in *that*?" Luke pointed at the screen that showed the water wild and dark.

Regan shrugged.

"Right. Time to get focused. I've asked Vincent to draft a list of the damage and to prioritise our tasks."

They worked through the list. The biggest concern was the aquaculture infrastructure. It looked like one of the fish pens had broken. That was months' worth of supply potentially gone. They wouldn't know about the oyster beds until they did a full inspection. The second greenhouse had also collapsed under the barrage of hail. Rylie hoped they didn't lose any more of their food supply. Rationing again was not going to be popular. They agreed they'd to wait to start repairs and onsite inspection, including accommodation and walkways, until the wind and rain had died down a little.

"In the meantime, let's get some food going." Rylie was feeling more grounded now that her team was in place, and they had some idea of the damage and work ahead. "Jerome, can you coordinate a working party in the kitchen to put out some soup or something?"

"Sure thing. We'll get those tummies filled, pronto."

"Actually, why don't the three of you go? Kate, Imo, Luke – you can help Jerome. Show a united front. Regan can stay here with me and Vincent to monitor sensors and comms."

"I need to get over to the aquaponics dock. Check it out." Regan made to get to his feet. Rylie pressed him back down again.

"You're not going anywhere. You're a loose cannon, and now a liability with an injury. So, no more hero antics from you, Regan Delarge. I need help here anyway."

He narrowed his eyes but said nothing.

The others made their way to the Nest's giant commercial kitchen, leaving Rylie and Regan with the display screens and Vincent, standing unblinking at attention.

Rylie clicked through the screens, but there was nothing new. The dark skies continued to disgorge its load of purging rain. It sluiced off surfaces. Rylie thanked the designers again for their foresight and careful drainage plans. Flooding on a floating island was a major concern. As was damage to the moorings in the storm, but they seemed to have escaped that so far. Satisfied that everything was as stable as it could be, Rylie turned to Regan, who sat leaning forward in his chair and watching the screens as she switched views.

"Have we got news from the mainland?" Regan asked.

"Good question. I haven't checked the news stream."

She swiped to a different display and the news reel came up.

"Oh God!" Rylie covered her mouth as images of widespread flooding, destroyed houses, fallen trees flashed on the screen.

Regan's face was grey and screwed tight in concern. "That's in Montreal. Far from the storm cell centre. If they're getting that kind of damage there, what is it like further north? The coastal towns not far from here?"

Rylie swiped a few more screens and put in a search. Nothing came up.

"Go to satellite images." His voice was uncharacteristically thin, and worry pulled his skin tight on his forehead.

They gasped. It looked like there was nothing left. Rylie tracked the satellite imagery down the coast of the Fleuve St Laurent. Roads were gone. Cars were sitting at weird angles where the water had carried them. At the small regional airports, it looked like someone had picked up the planes and played a game of jacks, leaving them sprawled and broken like discarded toys.

And there were bodies, too. They could see people washed up on the shoreline, strewn in front of buildings.

Regan went to his pile of belongings in the corner and pulled out his phone. He dialled one number. Then another.

"Nothing. It just signals busy."

"Telecommunications are probably down. Not surprising, given the damage."

"I've got to go."

"Whoa – wait. Go where?"

"I've got family out there." Regan coughed as emotion expanded in his throat and chest.

"All right. Slow down. You can't go out in the storm yet." Rylie stepped in front of Regan to block his exit. "Especially not with that injury." She spread her arms out to stop him as he tried to step past her.

"You can't drive a boat. Not with that arm. And certainly not in this weather." She put a hand gently on his chest. "We'll figure it out, all right? We can't go barrelling out the door without more information." He stopped moving and took a deep breath.

"You're right. Okay. More info. We need more info." He sat back down again and winced as he adjusted his arm sling.

"I'll see if I can get the Coast Guard. We have their satellite phone number." He nodded and waited. Rylie made the call on the Terra Blanca satellite phone.

"It's ringing," she said and smiled at Regan. "Yes, hello. Governor Rylie Addison here on Terra Blanca. What? No, we're not calling for support. We're actually okay. Our initial systems indicate we've managed to make it through. We're calling about rescue operations for the coastal towns up here. What's happening?"

She nodded and acknowledged what the operator was saying. "Have you got a list of survivors? Not yet? When will we get that?" She waited some more as the explanation came through.

"Can we take survivors?" She looked at Regan, whose face lit up. "I'll get back to you on that. We'll need to make an assessment of our accommodation and what we're capable of taking on. Yeah. No problem. We'll touch base in an hour." She hung up.

"They might be out there. We can bring them here – we've got room—"

"Who are we talking about?"

"Paloma. My ex. And Jay. My son."

"Oh, I'm so sorry, Regan. I hope they're all right. Where were they living?"

He pointed at one of the flattened villages on the coastline.

"I see. Well, hopefully they made it to safety before the storm hit. We'll know soon." Rylie patted his shoulder. It was rigid. His jaw was stiff.

"Did I see their names on the applications for the next round of residents?"

"Yeah."

"Were they going to live with you?"

"No." He glanced down. Rylie waited. She felt there was more. "I was hoping to reconcile. Eventually. This was one way of mending bridges. Get them here. Get a better life going for them. For all of us." He dashed a fist against the tears that rolled. He shook his head and looked away.

Rylie considered him, her heart swelling. She knew loss. Sometimes the best thing was to focus on something else. "We'll need to inspect accommodation. See what damage is there. The new accommodation platform isn't ready yet, but we might be able to fit some survivors there, too."

He nodded and coughed again as he wrangled his emotions.

"Why don't you gather some of the marine patrol team and organise an inspection of the accommodation platforms? It looks like the wind is easing. That will give us some information for the Coast Guard."

"Sure. Good idea." He stood and went to pull on his rain jacket. Rylie helped him do it up over his injured arm.

"As soon as I know anything, I'll let you know. I promise."

He smiled weakly. "Thank you, Rylie."

CHAPTER TWENTY-THREE

"ARE YOU SURE that's all the survivors we can take?" Rylie asked. She was hoping for a different answer. The councillors gathered in the storm-response war room after a full assessment of damage across Terra Blanca. Most residents had returned to their accommodation and submitted their list of repairs to be done. Broken windows, a few damaged and leaking roofs, and one walkway that had been ripped from its platform hinges. One of the boats had damage to its hull, a trout fish pen was torn open and most of the fish had escaped. The Vertical Farm had suffered in the hail, and they'd lost their salad crop for the month.

"Let's review it again. Kate, how many can we add to the new accommodation platform?"

"The platform is sound from a plumbing and power point of view. Ready for testing and set-up. All the residences are finished and functional. We don't have any of the amenities yet. They were ordered for next month's 3D printing round, once we'd finished the cosmetic touches. So, in theory, we could have the full three hundred sleeping berths filled, if people were happy to borrow pots, plates and so on from the current Terra Blancans."

"And, Jerome, how many can we feed, given the current supply?"

"We were only just getting close to full production when the storm hit."

"Thanks to all the donated muscle from various departments," added Imogen.

"Yeah, of course. Everyone pitched in. Good stuff." Jerome gave them all thumbs up. Regan grunted and Jerome added, "And, of course, Regan and his crew really put the boot in and ramped it up. Thanks, dude."

"So how many can we take, now, given the food supply?" Rylie reiterated.

"Since it looks like one of the trout farm pens is down, and with the damage we found in the Vertical Farm, we'll be back to the basics again. We can feed all current Terra Blancans on current production without going to reserves or rations. Any extras, and we will be on rations and reserves for at least six weeks until we can increase production in the insect farm and the lab-grown proteins."

"So, how many can we take, if we ration, and dip into reserves?"

Jerome rubbed his jaw and blew air into his cheeks as he thought. "We can probably take about a hundred. Our reserves could cover us for three months. They'd be ready to go home after that, right?"

"Who knows?" Imogen said. "It depends how badly their homes were destroyed. They might be here for a lot longer."

"Wait – what about the next Terra Blancan migrants?" Regan said. "We have three hundred people lined up and waiting for those berths. They were scheduled to move in September."

"I think it's fair to say our timelines and plans will need to be adjusted," Luke said. "Our first priority should be to help the survivors, don't you think?"

Regan gave him a hard look but did not answer.

"One hundred. Only one hundred," Rylie murmured. "So, it's just our food supply that's limiting us? If we got external supply, then we could take more?"

They all looked at her with surprise. Terra Blanca was a closed ecosystem. Imports risked bio-security. Besides, mainland supply was expensive and limited, given the drought and fires, and floods. Food would be scarce everywhere.

"What are you thinking, Rylie?" Kate asked.

"We might be able to get some non-perishables from somewhere. Disaster relief or something. That would allow us to take on more of the survivors."

"I think we should put that to a community vote," Regan said. "People need to know what our charity is costing us."

"What do you mean, Regan?" Luke said.

"Think about it. We will need to ration. We need to give up our reserves." Regan counted off the issues on his enormous fingers. "We will probably go back to adding shifts to food production. Imogen will lose her innovation team again. That will put the Dopplebots behind – again. Kate's team will need to work double time to do repairs and get the accommodation platforms ready. Plus, lots of people have family waiting to come on to those platforms. They may not like having to defer the next residents' arrival by another six to twelve months."

"I see. But don't you think most people would want to help if they could?" Luke said.

"I think we should ask." His voice was a low rumble.

"Agreed," added Rylie. "We can work with Vincent to calculate exactly how many people we can take, given the food production situation, and if we can get any additional supplies."

"If we can help, we should help," said Kate.

"Just as long as everyone knows the cost," said Regan.

CHAPTER TWENTY-FOUR

THE VOTE WAS not unanimous, but the majority carried the motion. They would take one hundred and seventy-five survivors. More, if they could find additional food supplies.

Rylie liaised extensively with the Coast Guard and disaster relief centre they'd set up near Quebec City. Kate and her team, along with people from Regan's team, worked doggedly to get the repairs done and the accommodation complete.

Regan had managed to get in contact with his ex-wife, Paloma. They had driven inland and sheltered at a school before the storm hit. They hadn't been back to their home yet as the roads were still impassable.

"Rylie," Regan said as he joined her in the storm recovery war room, two days after the community vote.

"Yes, Regan? How is the arm feeling?"

He was out of the sling. Luke's tests had confirmed it was just a nasty bruise. It was still swollen and very discoloured.

"It's all right. Hey, listen, I had an idea. Paloma and Jay are at one of the school shelters. Can we get them on the survivor list for Terra Blanca?"

Rylie sucked in her breath. It was the third conversation she'd had that day from Terra Blancan residents wanting to bump their families up on to the survivor list, instead of waiting for the next residential platform to be built.

"They're coming here later anyway. So, we'd be hitting two birds with one stone, so to speak."

He looked so hopeful, it crushed her spirit. Regan rarely showed any vulnerability, and this was important to him.

"I'm sorry, Regan, I can't make any promises. The Coast Guard is managing the list. They are evaluating each person on a case-by-case basis. Not much I can do."

He pressed his lips together and narrowed his gaze.

"You got anyone on the mainland, Rylie?"

"No. It's just me and Eve now."

"So, you know, then."

"Know what?"

"That you'd do anything to stay together. When that's all you've got."

His blue eyes held hers with an intensity that seemed to bore into the back of her skull.

"I tell you what, Regan. I'll speak to them again and ask them if they could keep Paloma and Jay in mind."

He held her gaze. Then he nodded and left.

Rylie sighed. She just couldn't please everyone. She'd already negotiated three names on that list, Eve's old boyfriend and his parents. Their eligibility was a stretch. They'd been in Montreal, so not technically in the worst-hit areas.

This was the only way they'd make it into Terra Blanca as their application for residency in the next round had been rejected. They just didn't need the skills of a pilot or a real estate agent. The focus now was on self-sufficiency, infrastructure, and the fledgling tech company and the Dopplebots.

Rylie had thought deeply about this favour for Eve. Her daughter had nurtured her bitterness into a deep-seated resentment since they left the old town. Eve had never wanted to leave, and did not want the isolated life on Terra Blanca, even if it meant better living conditions in the end. And then, when it was obvious Rylie was not going to turn down the governor role, Eve had campaigned relentlessly to get Jared and his parents included with the next round of settlers. It was exhausting to keep saying no. And to withstand the constant criticism that came as a result.

If she could make this happen for Eve, then it would be one less burden to carry. She'd been discreet with the Coast Guard about her request, so there was little likelihood of that blowing back on her. She definitely didn't need that headache on top of everything else.

CHAPTER TWENTY-FIVE

THE SURVIVORS ARRIVED in a jumble. Regan and Imogen, along with their teams, helped settle the new arrivals on the second accommodation platform. They'd managed to fill all three hundred berths since the Coast Guard had brought reserve supplies as donations. Paloma and Jay, Regan's family, were not among them.

The current Terra Blancans loaned their cutlery and crockery, bedding, and clothes to the newcomers. There was a burgeoning sense of compassion and care for one another.

Until the donated reserves ran out.

The Nest clamoured with unrest. All the Terra Blancan residents gathered in protest at the latest round of rationing. Half supplies had been allocated. All able-bodied residents were working extra shifts in food production. There had been several injuries in the aquaculture sector because the training had been rushed for the survivors. On top of that, someone had been raiding reserves, and the word had gotten out.

Rylie raised her arms in supplication, trying to quieten them.

"We need more food!"

"We're starving!"

Rylie moved around the mic to make it reverberate. The high-pitched squeal cut through the cries.

"Let me address the issues," she said in a booming voice. "Yes, we've cut the rations. It's only to make sure we have enough in the next few weeks. Thanks to the extra hands from the newcomers, we'll be able to start ramping up supply again. In the meantime, I've been working on getting us some more external supplies."

Murmurs at that, Rylie noted. It was the hardest promise to deliver on. There just wasn't any extra food in the supply chain. All of it went to the existing mainland survivor camps. Terra Blanca was considered a luxury resort in comparison.

"How long are the newcomers going to stay? I've got family lined up to take their spot. As per the original contract."

Rylie breathed deeply. This was a huge, contentious issue. "The mainlanders are working as fast as possible to rebuild houses, roads. It's not a fast process, as you can imagine. As soon as there is somewhere to go to, our newcomers will be able to go."

"Is it true some are being offered permanent housing here?"

"There's nothing set in stone. There's a lot of variables at play—"

"I don't believe it. They just swan in and get it handed to them. Don't even need to apply. Don't even need to sign up to the Terra Blanca Charter."

"Hang on a minute! No final decisions have been made. A lot depends on reconstruction, as I said. Look, we are doing our best to feed and house everyone, to keep everyone safe."

"Fat lot of good that does my family, waiting in squalor, in a storm-refugee camp, for their place here."

Backward and forward it went. Eventually, Rylie consulted Jerome and they agreed to add to people's rations for the week.

"But since there have been raids on the reserves, we will be instigating a guard on the supply shed until further notice. I am sorry it had to come to this."

CHAPTER TWENTY-SIX

RYLIE RAN HER hand through her hair as she stared at Vincent. She puffed her cheeks and sighed.

"Are you sure we can't work some other angle?" she said.

"What about the American supplier? Maybe they can help?" Luke added.

Rylie and Luke had been working on the supply issue while the rest of the councillors managed repairs and doubled down on food production and security. There had been several skirmishes lately in the supply lines as people waited for their weekly rations. Regan and his crew had also found several more smuggling stashes. Off-island visits were banned again, and tensions were running high.

"I've worked it through with Athena," Vincent said. "No other supplier will distribute to us. They have back-orders to fill for other storm camps, and we're too small. We simply don't have enough purchase power to make it worth their while."

"Maybe we can talk them down a notch, Rylie," Luke said. "If we give NutriFusion all the places on the third residential platform, even if we insist they follow our skills-requirement process and we handle the selection, that's still going to upset current Terra Blancans."

"They were pretty firm on it, Luke. We give them three hundred spots or they walk."

"Their compassion is heart-warming."

"The only other choice was Source Foods. And they wanted a controlling share of the Dopplebot production."

"Maybe we should do that."

"What? And give up our future prosperity and a critical economic asset?"

"It might be better than the hell storm that will erupt when we give up three hundred places to NutriFusion."

Rylie pursed her lips and touched her owl necklace. There was no easy way through.

"Even with the NutriFusion deal, it won't be enough supply. We'll probably have to do the Source Food deal, too." Rylie frowned. "A delay for the Terra Blancan families is not ideal. But they'll get over it. It's just a delay to the waitlist, not an elimination."

"I am not sure Regan will see it that way, Rylie."

She thought about the big man and the tears he had shed for his ex-wife and young son. Her heart panged. What was she to do? The residents and survivors were at each other's throats, they were all hungry and exhausted, and Regan's stern security measures were stirring up the objectors again. They needed food. And they needed to hold on to their economic sovereignty. They needed to wear this short-term inconvenience for a long-term win.

"Vincent, what are some possible outcomes if we go with the NutriFusion deal?" she asked.

"Once they made their deliveries, reserves would be re-stocked. Rationing could be eased until food production could be met, in approximately three weeks. The rabble would chill."

"Three weeks! That's all we'd need and we'd be out of the woods," she said.

"What are some other consequences of this decision, Vincent?" Luke asked.

"If NutriFusion keeps control of selection for the next three hundred residents, then we risk not having the right skills to run the community."

"So, we insist on maintaining that component," Rylie said. "Anything else?"

"There are two hundred and eighty-one Terra Blancan family members offshore registered and approved for the next accommodation platform. This agreement, in addition to the survivor resettlement plan, will push back their residency by close to two years. They won't be happy."

"Two years," Luke gasped. "How many Terra Blancan residents does that affect?"

"There are one hundred and five Terra Blancan residents with family approved and waiting."

"About a third of the original residents," murmured Rylie.

"Maybe we should take this to a direct vote, Rylie?"

Rylie looked back at Luke and saw the strain on his face.

"And ask them to vote between starving and saving their loved ones from their current predicament? No thanks. We're the council. I'm the governor. I was granted negotiation rights in last week's community vote to get us supply. So, I'm getting us supply."

She rubbed her forehead.

"Your call, your head, Rylie," Luke said.

"Athena, get me NutriFusion then Source Food on the holo display. I'm ready to negotiate."

CHAPTER TWENTY-SEVEN

REGAN PRESSED REPLAY for the third time on the Nest council tapes. He watched as Rylie gave away three hundred places on Terra Blanca. Gave away his family's future. His future. His chance of happiness and reconciliation with Paloma. He struggled to swallow the lump in his throat.

He let the recording run through, soaked in his grief for his lost family. Two years! They had two more years of struggling while he was here, making promises Rylie broke.

He was about to end the recording when he heard it.

"Athena, play that again. Start from one minute ago."

Regan watched as Rylie commanded Athena to dial up Source Foods. Luke was there beside her, rubbing his goatee.

"Henri. Yes. We'll take it. Only twenty per cent, though. We're not giving you any more of the Dopplebots. When can you deliver?"

Regan's brain fizzed with horror. Rylie had just traded one of their key assets. And she hadn't told anyone.

He checked his memory from that morning. She had announced the NutriFusion deal with the three hundred places. He remembered that clearly. There was an uproar. He'd been as shocked as everyone else. Two years until he could have his son, Jay, with him.

But did she disclose the Source Food Dopplebot agreement? He couldn't remember exactly, he was so upset.

His phone buzzed.

"Marty. What is it?"

"Regan. You've got to get down here. We found the mother lode of contraband. And I think I know who's been smuggling."

Source Food and the Dopplebots would have to wait.

CHAPTER TWENTY-EIGHT

REGAN MADE HIS way to the dock where Marty and a couple of the young workers were poking at the latest discovery.

"How goes, boys?" Regan said. "What's going on?"

"Hey, Regan. We've got ourselves a real haul this time," Marty said with a flourish. "I've just opened the first barrel and it's full of cheese."

There were four other barrels. "Shall we take a look?" Regan said.

Marty prised one of them open.

"No way!" the younger one said.

"I can't freaking believe it!" said the older one.

Oh my God, thought Regan. *It's a roast. An actual lamb roast.* His mouth started salivating at the thought of it. This must've cost an absolute bomb. He didn't know where they were growing and processing meat. And here it was now, a feast fit for kings.

"And that's not all, Regan. Take a look at this." Marty passed Regan a scrap of paper.

Hey E! Hope all is well with you and J. Thanks as always for the biz. Latest Dopplebot info very useful. M

"That's bloody Eve Addison, I'm sure of it. She's always going around with that Jared kid. One of the storm survivors who arrived with his parents."

Regan's eyes opened wide as Marty shared a triumphant look.

"The governor's own daughter. What do you think of that, Regan?" Marty prodded.

"You think the governor is in on it too?" one of the younger boys asked.

"I wouldn't be surprised," Marty said. "She's always so defensive of little Miss Eve."

Regan stared at the slip of paper again. All this time chasing smugglers and it was Eve. Right under the governor's nose. And she was trading Dopplebot secrets for contraband?

What to do with this information?

Regan's head pounded. This was a lot to take in. First NutriFusion stole his family's place on Terra Blanca, then Source Foods got a slice of the Dopplebots, and now the governor's daughter was operating a smuggling operation and trading corporate secrets.

"Let me do some more investigating," Regan said at last. "We don't want to run around half-cocked."

"What about all this contraband?"

"Put it back where you found it."

The men looked disappointed.

"Look, this is the biggest find we've had yet. All the

other stuff has been a little bit here and there, with no consistent stash site. For something this big, the smuggler, if it's Eve, must have been confident it wouldn't get discovered. Which means she's likely used it before with smaller deliveries." Regan rubbed his jaw as he thought.

"Just keep this to yourselves for now. Don't tell anyone about the contraband. Or who we suspect. If it is little Miss Eve, we will need a little more evidence. If she thinks she's got a good haul stash site, she'll go again."

"All right then, will do."

"Marty, you and the boys set up surveillance on the stash site. I want to know who comes to get it, what happens to it. The lot."

"Roger that, boss."

The bait was set. They'd have their answers soon.

Regan wondered why he did not feel more elated.

Instead, a gnawing sense of dread filled his gut.

CHAPTER TWENTY-NINE

REGAN RETURNED TO the Nest and found a private conference room. Something niggled the back of his brain. Something about the list of survivors.

"Athena, please bring up the list of survivors we accepted," he instructed the A.I.

The list sprang up on the display.

"Sort by their residential address. By postcode, please."

The data re-organised. Regan scanned the data but didn't see anything that leapt out at him.

"What was the criteria the Canadian Rescue Service used to select survivors for Terra Blanca?"

"According to the agreement with the Provincial government, Terra Blanca was to take rural survivors first, in the most affected towns," Athena said.

"Are there any survivors who were outside these zones?"

"Affirmative. Three."

"Show me."

There they were.

Jared Dubois, Pascal Dubois, Yvette Dubois. Of Montreal. Nowhere near the rural towns where the other survivors were listed.

He recognised Jared's face. Eve's boyfriend. They'd been inseparable since the flood survivors had arrived.

E and J from the note.

He stared at the screen. The knot in his stomach grew heavier.

"What is the status of the survivors in relation to their application for Terra Blancan residency?"

"Sixty-two per cent have been approved. Thirty-three per cent have been denied. The remainder intend to return to their homes."

"And the Dubois family. What is their status?" He could barely say it.

"Approved."

"Show me their application and assessment records."

The form read: "Qualifications: Real Estate Agent and Pilot – not required. Status of application: Exception granted. Signed by: Rylie Addison, Imogen Bussle, Kate Watkins, The Terra Blanca residency subcommittee."

Regan felt sick. His head roared with fury.

Rylie had made an exception for her daughter's boy-friend's family. Fudged the community rules. And Imogen and Kate were in on it. While his family were left aside. For two years. Even after he'd asked. Practically begged.

And the deal with NutriFusion and Source Foods. Luke was in on that with Rylie.

What the hell is happening?

His phone buzzed. It was Marty.

"Yeah?"

"We got her!" Marty whispered. "All on camera, too. She's there with the boyfriend, right now, pulling it out from under the rock platform where we found it."

Regan rubbed his forehead.

"All right. Let it ride. Follow them. See where they take it. And who they take it to."

"Roger that."

Regan put his phone down.

This is not right. This has to stop.

After a moment, he picked up his phone again and started making calls.

Time for justice.

But first there was someone he needed to talk to.

CHAPTER THIRTY

JEROME WAS SITTING at the Vertical Farm staff kitchen table chatting to some of the crew when Regan appeared. Jerome jumped up.

"Regan. How are you, man? We were just taking a break."

The others had already stood and were cleaning away their coffee cups in a hurry.

"Jerome, can I have a word?"

"If it's about the insect protein flour, we've asked the tech to review the recipe and adjust the inputs."

"It's not about the crickets."

"And the carrots – our next crop is ready next week. Just a week late."

"It's not the carrots, either. Just shut up for a second."

"Okay, yeah. Sure. What is it?"

"Listen, did you know about the NutriFusion deal?"

"What? No. I mean, I found out when everyone else did."

"Your mother's on the mainland, waiting for residency, right?"

"Yeah." Jerome's jovial face sagged.

"Listen, you need to know something." Regan glanced around and then stepped closer to Jerome. "Rylie has been using governor privilege to boost people from the survivors list to full residency. Without passing the eligibility test. And she did it for her daughter's boyfriend and his family."

"No. Surely that can't be right?"

"I saw it for myself. I read the assessment form. Kate and Imogen co-signed it."

"What? Kate? Imo? No." He shook his head and took a step backwards.

"Jerome, listen to me. The council is out of control. Those three are signing off on people who shouldn't even get a look-in. And then there's Luke."

"What about Luke?" Jerome looked frightened now.

"He was there when Rylie negotiated the Source Foods and NutriFusion deals. I don't know what his deal is, but he's helping Rylie give away all of what's great about Terra Blanca."

"Why are you telling me all this, man? You've never included me in anything before. You don't even like me! Is this some sort of trap?"

"Jerome, it's true I've had it in for you. I really thought you were screwing up the Vertical Farm. But then I had a go and… well…"

"Well, what?"

Regan paused for a few heartbeats and then sighed. "Well, it's not as easy as it looks," he admitted, finally.

"Thank you." Jerome looked pleased.

"You're still a slutty bimbo and a sloppy dresser with an art for slacking."

"Seriously, dude? And just when I thought you were trying to be friends."

"I don't want to be your friend, Jerome."

Jerome snorted. "That's clear."

"What I do want is justice. Look, your mother, and my family, are wasting away on the mainland where it's hot, cramped, and nasty. Rylie and her cronies have squeezed them out. We've got to stop this craziness."

"Well, this is going to make the dinner party awkward, isn't it?"

"What dinner party?"

"You don't know?"

"What are you talking about?"

"I thought you knew."

"Knew what?"

"Rylie is having a celebration dinner with the councillors tomorrow night. Because of the supply deal and all that."

"Oh." Regan felt a jolt. "I see." He'd been left out. Deliberately. His cheeks burned.

"I guess that means Rylie never asked you about the contraband."

Regan's gaze narrowed and this time it was Jerome's face that flushed red.

"What contraband?"

"The contraband you confiscated a few days ago. She

said she didn't want to put it up for lottery this time because people were being crazy in the supply lines. She didn't want to add fuel to the fire."

"So... she's just taking it? For a dinner party?"

Jerome shrugged.

"Unbelievable." Regan fumed and rubbed his face. "There's something *you* should know, Jerome."

"What's that?"

"Eve is the smuggler."

"You have got to be kidding! You're pulling my leg, right?"

"I most certainly am not. Eve has been smuggling and dealing food with the survivors, with the help of her queue-jumping boyfriend."

"Well, holy shit."

"It's worse. I think she's been selling Dopplebot secrets to fund the transactions."

Jerome's jaw dropped. He just gawped at Regan.

"This whole thing is messed up. We've got to set it straight. Who knows what they'll negotiate next. Listen, I've got an idea. You want in?"

Jerome crossed his arms and considered Regan's earnest face.

"What do you have in mind?"

"We're going to take back Terra Blanca."

CHAPTER THIRTY-ONE

REGAN GLANCED AT the faces in the dim light of the dock shed. Marty had spread the word and curiosity had brought his mainstay supporters to hear what was urgent, and secret. Regan knew this group was struggling more than most on Terra Blanca. People like him, with families, who'd had their residency applications pushed back by two years. Due to the survivors and the latest supply deal with NutriFusion.

"Listen up, folks." He raised his hands to get attention. He towered above them and they fell silent.

"Today we found something disturbing." He paused for dramatic effect. "The council has been violating the community code. Today I discovered that the governor, along with Imogen and Kate, used their positions of privilege to accept survivors who were not on the priority list. Three of these survivors just happen to be the governor's daughter's boyfriend and his family."

The crowd murmured and scowled.

"And I also found out that this very same family has been accepted by the subcommittee for long-term residency, despite the fact they do not fit the criteria. So, while *your* families, and *my* family, are left to fend in dire straits, even *with* the right qualifications, the governor and her cronies have seen fit to accept a real estate agent and a pilot.

"Now, I can understand doing your daughter a favour. But when you add that to the NutriFusion deal, which sets up a corporate monopoly over residency, and selling off a stake in the Dopplebots, what I see is dereliction of duty and abuse of power. It grieves me to say it but it seems obvious that the council is not fit for duty and must be stopped. Immediately."

There were some nods.

"We can vote them from office," someone offered.

"There's more." Regan took a big, reluctant breath. "We've discovered who the smuggler is. It's Eve Addison. She and Jared have been running the trade for a band of survivors."

"What the hell? The governor's daughter?"

"We suspect she has been selling Dopplebot technology to fund the contraband."

The outrage was palpable. They'd suffered lockdowns, inspections, off-island visit bans, rations, extra work shifts to get the food production operating, and having to watch their own family members continue to struggle on the mainland. And the governor, and the other council members, were using their positions of power to look after her daughter. And likely turning a blind eye to the smuggling and corporate betrayal.

"There's one more thing."

They fell quiet quickly this time.

"The governor is hosting a dinner party tonight. With the other councillors. Well. *Most* of the other councillors. Obviously, *I* wasn't invited."

Eyes fixed on him now.

"On the menu? The contraband we seized a few days ago. Contraband the governor's own daughter snuck onshore."

"Jesus effing Christ!"

"That's too much."

"How dare they!"

"Why do they get the contraband? What happened to the lottery?"

After weeks of rations, and even with the promise of additional supplies coming with the NutriFusion and Source Foods deals, this jangled nerves like nothing else.

"So, my question to you is: are we going to stand for this? We've been working our butts off to provide for this community. And what do we get? Criticism. Disdain. We get overlooked and sidelined for corporate interests and nepotism!" Regan spat his words as his rage unleashed.

"They take what they want for themselves. They use the system for their own personal ends. It's time for new leadership! We can't let these corrupt powermongers captain the ship anymore! We need good, hard-working, honest people at the helm! We need to take control of the government and put things right! Are you with me?" There was a roar of approval. "Then let's put things right! Here's what we're going to do."

They spent the next few hours discussing the best approach to challenge the council. They needed to secure the main centres of Terra Blanca. Jerome would lock down the Vertical Farm and the various food supply sheds with his crew and prevent access to the reserve supply if anyone wanted to raid them in protest. Also on high priority was the comms tower and the Innovation Hub so they could control the communications off-island until they were ready.

They made a list of troublemakers and a plan to neutralise them. Someone had the list of the original "objectors" to Regan's management when he was in charge of the Vertical Farm and they started identifying ring leaders they needed to contain. People who weren't fans of Regan and might put up a fight. Chief among them was Luke Finnegan. Meddlesome twat.

As they worked through the plan, the outrage turned to bitterness. There was a heated resolve with a unified focus: take control.

"Justice Squad, it's time. Let's take back Terra Blanca and set things right!" Regan clapped a few on the back as his nerves tightened. He marched out of the shed with his crew seething beside him.

He didn't suggest what came next; it happened on its own. People grabbed a shovel, a stick, a broom. Makeshift weapons. Regan had a moment of concern, but then figured it might help them feel a little more confident if they had something to wave at people. Funny how something in your hand made you feel more in charge. More powerful. More alive!

They neared Governor Rylie's cabin. The sound of laughter coming from his fellow councillors drifted out of an open window, and his heart skipped a beat. Then he set his resolve.

No turning back now.

PART THREE

CHAPTER THIRTY-TWO

ONCE THE COUNCILLORS were secure, Regan and his crew headed to the council offices around the rim of the Nest. There was some initial resistance, but his gang seemed to have it under control now.

Regan went to the council kitchen. That's where he hit another jackpot. Sausages still warm in a pan. Sausages!

No way! They were hiding the contraband in the damn council kitchen! Hidden in plain sight. He and his marine patrol officers hadn't thought to check the council kitchen.

He crammed a sausage dripping with tomato sauce into his mouth. Greasy mess dribbled down his chin. He licked his fingers with his cheeks still bulging and snuffle-grunted in delight. Real sausages. Made from actual pigs. That must have cost a fortune, he thought.

So, this is where they've been hiding the good stuff. That Eve bitch is a sneaky, two-faced, talking head. Regan glanced around the coolroom, its shelves loaded with the community's supplies. There were probably other little stashes tucked away in here, too. No more of that now! Terra Blanca was going to be restored. He would see to it. Return proper law and order. No more stupid objectors. All that blathering – huge waste of time. So many people up themselves and needing to have a say.

They like the sound of their own voices is what that is, he thought. No more endless babble now. They had a community to run. People just needed to do what they were told and it would all get done. He knew. He'd run teams before. He'd run successful companies. You just needed someone in charge. A firm hand at the tiller. They'd see. It would all settle down soon enough. A few people had been hurt when they'd seized the Nest, but not too badly, he hoped. It was all kinds of crazy. Everything had happened so fast.

Some of his crew had been a little rough. He'd have to clamp down on that. No sense in beating people into submission. That wouldn't help their cause. He'd have to do a little sweet talking to set it right again.

He'd make a show of that meddler, Luke Finnegan. Stupid troublemaker. He started all this drama in the first place. Objector number one. Always challenging him. The nerve! Finnegan needled everyone with criticisms. Regan had just got Governor Rylie all sweet on his ideas and damn Finnegan upset the apple cart. Threw it all into chaos. If they would just follow his advice, Terra Blanca would run just fine. Him in charge, Governor Addison as a puppet, and all would be cool. First order of business: he'd review the damn settlement list. He'd put the layabouts to work – no more skiving off. Everyone had to pull their weight around here. A bit of punishment would be the right incentive.

That was Finnegan's first objection: punishment as incentive didn't work. *Sure as shit it did!* Regan had seen many a lazy team whipped into shape with a bit of retribution hanging over their heads. People liked rules. A bit of discipline. It helped them to know where they stood. All this waffly talk just made people confused. And where there was confusion, there was chaos.

Regan looked around for something to wipe his hands on. Nothing on the counters. *Even the tea towels are full of subterfuge,* he thought. *Nothing is what you think it is on this goddamn island.* He shrugged and wiped the grease on his shirt front. He'd wash it out later.

Right now, he had a job to do. He had the governor and her whimpering pile of bootlickers locked up and that upstart irritant, Luke Finnegan, isolated and under control too. He'd better get the Justice Squad to pull their heads in. He could hear the shouts and screams of the Terra Blancans rising another pitch.

"Marty!" Regan yelled.

He heard a scuffle and shouts down the corridor. Regan strode to the door with his baton in hand. "Marty!"

The blood-spattered face of his offsider appeared at the far end of the corridor.

"I'm here!" he panted.

"What the hell, Marty! What happened to peaceful persuasion? You're covered in blood."

"They were resisting. I tackled one of the survivors who was yelling and causing trouble. We fell. He split his lip and spat on me."

"Well, take it easy, would you? Remind the others to take it down a notch for Chrissake. Get the squad together.

Tell them to pull back to the council rooms at the Nest. Leave guards on Finnegan and the governor and her crew. I'll meet you there in ten."

"Roger that."

"And, Marty—"

"Yeah?"

"Tell Delaware to hustle and get that comms blocker happening. I saw some people streaming with their holos."

"On it, boss." Marty sprang back along the corridor.

Regan smiled to himself. The comms blocker was a radical new tech he'd brought with him originally. He still had good contacts on the outside who were willing to help out an old buddy. Favours were the best form of currency these days.

Regan took another look in the community kitchen coldroom. He stuffed more sausages in a pocket for later and shoved the remnants of a cake slice into his salivating maw.

Uprisings were hungry work.

CHAPTER THIRTY-THREE

ONCE SHE WRIGGLED through the window, Rylie made a beeline for the communications tower. They had to get a message out. She stayed in the shadows and crept behind buildings. The insurrectionists were everywhere.

As she got nearer to the satellite tower, she heard a noise behind her. She whipped around to see someone waving madly at her from behind a door. The man opened it a crack and signalled to come over urgently. Rylie dashed over and the man let her in.

"Quick!" He grabbed her and pulled her inside and shut the door quickly behind them.

"Are you okay?" he asked, looking her over.

"Yes, I'm fine. Thanks."

"You're safe here, as long as you don't go out. They're guarding the comms tower pretty fiercely and running people off if they dare to approach. My buddy Squirrel just got his head punched in. They've got him locked up in there."

"Squirrel?" Rylie asked.

"Yeah. Nickname. He eats like a squirrel." He put his hands up to his mouth as if nibbling on nuts. "I'm Sean, by the way." The man thrust his hand out.

"Rylie." She shook his hand.

"I know who you are, Governor. I heard you were all locked up?"

"We were. I mean, still are. I escaped. The others are still locked in my cabin. Look, Sean, was it?" He nodded. "I need your help. I need to get into that tower to get the comms back up."

"Are you crazy?" he said. "Those terrorists will jump you the moment you go anywhere near the tower."

"Could you distract them for me? How many of them are there?"

"I've seen at least two. They're hanging out in the stairwell most of the time. They wait for people to open the door and then jump them."

Rylie thought for a moment. "We'll need some help, then. Are you in contact with anyone? Can you rally some assistance?"

Sean thought for a moment. "I know there's a bunch of people holed up at the Wellness Centre. We could send a message with my drone. I do coastline surveillance for search and rescue. Some of them would likely help out. It's not far from here."

Sean sprang into action, excited by the prospect of doing something constructive. Rylie stayed by the window and watched the door of the comms tower. It was lit by a security globe. The door to the tower swung open and two men emerged. Both were holding what looked like paddles. Dockworkers.

One man guarded the door while the other went around the corner. He came back zipping up his trousers and then stood guard while his friend went to relieve himself in turn.

There were no windows in the building. The only access was through the front door. That was their only chance to take control. They could seize them when they came out for another piss. How long did it take for people to need a pee? A couple of hours, she guessed. It was just after midnight, so they still had lots of night left to spring a trap. That would give Sean enough time to get the people at the Wellness Centre to come over. Assuming they would dare.

Sean stayed glued to his drone navigation screen. He guided it to the Wellness Centre and set it down at the front door. After what seemed like ages to Rylie, the drone's camera showed the door opening and a face peering down at the machine.

"Come on! Grab the note!" Sean muttered. It wasn't a delivery drone, so he'd taped a message to the hull.

The person's hands reached for the drone and stepped back with the note in hand. They leaned back to get some light from the interior and then called out to someone behind the door. A few more faces appeared, and a conversation ensued. The first person stared down at the drone and raised a finger to indicate to wait a minute. He disappeared and after what seemed like an interminable amount of time, came back with a piece of paper. He put it up to the screen. Sean and Imogen read, "We will send some people to help. Meet at 4am, two streets back from the tower. Careful of patrol."

"Patrol. I haven't seen a patrol around here. The rebels must have more people than we thought. I'll move the drone off the street for now."

The drone's camera lifted away from the doorway and Sean guided it to a perch across the street. They could see the Wellness Centre's access and much of the street now. Still no sign of the patrol.

Rylie and Sean resumed their vigilance at the window.

The night dragged on and on. Rylie stretched and rolled her shoulders as the muscles in her back ached from the strain of constant surveillance. She looked at her watch, realising that they had been waiting for almost four hours now. She was starting to get impatient.

"Sean, are there any signs of movement from the drone camera?"

"Nothing. Not sure where these patrols are but they are not around the Wellness Centre."

"We've got about thirty minutes before we need to meet them. Do you think our plan will work?"

"I think so. When they come out for a pee, we'll grab one of them and distract the other one while you slip in to reconnect the comms."

"Perfect. What could go wrong?" she said with a crooked smile.

"Hey look! They're on their way!" he said. The drone display showed about half a dozen people sneaking out of the Wellness Centre.

"You track them on the way over. I'll go get in position."

Sean nodded in agreement. Time to make a move. She slipped over to the door and opened it a crack. Still no movement at the tower. Her heart pounded and filled her senses with adrenaline.

"Rylie!" Sean whispered loudly as she was about take a step. She closed the door quickly and looked back at him.

"Be careful."

She blinked at the concern on his face, nodded, turned back quickly, and slipped into the night. She needed to get around the back of the comms building, hiding in the shadows of trees and shrubs. She ran as quickly as she could, bent over low, praying she was small enough to be missed by a casual observer. She sprinted across the last stretch of open grass to the dark shadows at the back of the comms tower. She made it. Her heart hammered in her chest. It reminded her of a young rooster she had once caught escaping its pen. She'd grappled with the bird until she had it pinned under her arm. Its heart had thumped against her in terror like a frenzied mechanical hammer. Like he knew he was meant for the slaughterhouse.

Rylie breathed through the adrenaline, willing her nerves to calm. Her hands shook. Still, she waited. Where were the others? They should be here by now! The guards could be coming out for toilet break any moment.

Then she heard it. A stick snapping, bushes rustling. She got down low to the building and peered around the corner. She saw a glint of something and dark shapes in the shrubbery. Sean and the crew had arrived.

Another noise caught her attention. It sounded like the door to the comms building swinging open. She imagined one of the guards holding it open for the other as they had done before. Footsteps crunched against the grass, paused, and then the sound of liquid spraying against the building. The man sighed and farted.

Rylie pressed herself against the building, her senses straining. Then she heard a rush, a cry, and muffled grappling.

Rylie stood up slowly, her muscles tense and ready for action. She crept along the other side of the building. The second guard would be waiting for his companion and growing anxious.

"François? You there?"

The silence deepened.

"François?" The guard's voice was anxious.

Rylie trembled and breathed softly through flared nostrils, trying to calm herself.

"Ah, shit, François. Quit playing around."

The night held its breath.

Rylie heard the guard's tentative steps where François had gone. Now was her chance.

She sneaked along the side, ready to breach the front door. Just as she reached for the handle, she heard the surprised cries of the second guard as he was tackled and subdued by Sean and his allies. Her heart pounded in her chest as she took a deep breath, turned the handle with a shaking hand, and pushed the door open.

She stepped inside, her eyes scanned the room for any signs of movement. It was dark and quiet, but she could make out the shapes of various machines and equipment. She crept forward.

Suddenly, she heard a noise from behind a nearby door. Rylie spun as it swung open, a figure emerged wielding something large and brought it down on her head.

Everything went black.

CHAPTER THIRTY-FOUR

LUKE FINNEGAN STRETCHED his arms out in front and rolled his head side to side. He was stiff from sleeping on the floor in the meeting room they'd thrown him in. A day ago? He'd lost sense of time.

They'd split up the council once they worked out Rylie had escaped. He wondered how the others were doing. Kate would be panicking and complaining. Imogen would be trying to take down anyone who came near her. Eve? Probably taking notes for her grand exposé once things settled.

These guys are thugs, he thought. *All their grand talk about creating a better world. It was all bullshit. At the end of the day, they are just like people everywhere: selfish pricks.*

It turns out people don't overcome their basic nature that easily.

Luke thought about his secret employer. She was right to test the system. She must have known. She must have had her doubts. Otherwise, why send him here to stir up trouble?

Luke rubbed his chin. The stubble around his goatee was irritating. Scratching it made him itchier everywhere. He was still wearing the same jeans and shirt he'd been in the night it all started.

The night Regan Delarge incited a mob. *What a dick. Damn him!* Now he was stuck in this room, with a proverbial axe over his head. At least they let him out to take a piss. Such benevolence.

If only he could send a message out somehow to Maja. He regretted their arrangement of strictly no comms.

I wonder if she's getting this news feed, he thought. Surely, she'd be paying attention? She would notice there had been a comms lockdown on Terra Blanca once the trouble started. Was it Governor Rylie Addison who did that? She probably didn't want the fledgling community's reputation damaged.

Too late for that now. Regan Delarge is "at large". Luke smiled. At least he was maintaining his sense of humour.

Wasn't he?

Luke felt a twang of unease. He didn't like that sensation. He was used to feeling in control. And things were definitely out of his control right now. Where had it gone wrong, exactly?

Regan Delarge. If he was one of Maja's agents, he'd overworked the brief. She'd said to "challenge the system", not destroy it.

Was insurrection part of Regan's brief and Luke hadn't known about it?

In any case, Delarge was running his own game now. Only time would tell how it turned out.

"Finnegan!"

Luke jumped as someone hammered on the door.

"Wake up, Finnegan. It's show time!"

CHAPTER THIRTY-FIVE

"You're joking, right?" Huw's face was ashen, his eyes wide.

"No. I am not," Maja replied.

"You really did this? You actually organised – paid – for Luke Finnegan to go in and intentionally sabotage Terra Blanca?" His lips trembled.

"I did not ask him to 'sabotage'. I sent him as an agent. I suggested he challenge the system. I wanted to test the governance process and leadership maturity of the governor and council. I was worried that technocracy would fail. Luke was there as a check and stress tester. To intervene if things were not going well."

"Well, they are certainly not going well now. Looks like his stress testing failed spectacularly. Where was the check on this riot? And – why do it in such a – such an under-handed way? Why not be open about it?" Huw sputtered.

"It wouldn't be much of a test then, would it?" Maja fiddled with the hem of her silk jacket. "It had to be real."

"But how real is it to send in a saboteur? That doesn't make sense."

"Again, he was not a saboteur. He's an agent. And it made sense to me at the time."

Huw rubbed his jaw.

"Maja – why did you not come to me with this? Why not ask me my opinion? We're business partners!"

Maja looked out the window of the Gaia Enterprises training centre headquarters. The latest group of world designers was in session on the lawn in the shade, before it got too hot.

"This was a human development experiment, not a world design one. I thought it best to keep it private. For the sake of the experiment."

"If you'll excuse me, Maja, that's bullshit. This has a direct impact on Gaia. And on me. If anyone finds out this mess was caused by a secret agent that you planted – you, the great and celebrated world designer, Maja Garcia, this could sink us. Our business is successful due to the promise of better social harmony. And look at what's happening – people are being beaten up, held hostage, and who knows what else is happening there right now in this siege."

Maja pursed her lips. "That's just it. We don't know what's happening on the ground. We don't even know if this was Luke's doing or not. All I've got is that quick message from Rylie saying Luke was one of the 'objectors'. We don't know what they are, who they are, and what is actually happening."

Huw took a deep breath and blew it out while staring at the ceiling.

"Does anyone else know about this?"

"You mean the insurrection?"

"No – everyone with a holo-feed knows about the insurrection! I mean Luke Finnegan."

"Not that I know of. There was an explicit clause in the contract to maintain absolute secrecy. No discussion of this with anyone, and no communication between us once he arrived at Terra Blanca."

"What? There's a contract? An actual paper trail? Oh my God."

"It's encrypted."

"And you think that's going to stop a motivated hacker? Oh my God, Maja! This gets worse and worse. We need to bury that contract deep. No one must ever find out about this, do you hear?"

Maja looked uncomfortable. "I think we need to be accountable. It's not ethical to—"

"Ethical! There is nothing ethical about this at all. From the start. You planted a saboteur – sorry, 'agent' – and now a whole community is in jeopardy and people are being injured. And now – now you're going to find some ethics? Give me a break." He turned away from her, the disgust radiating plainly in his voice.

He looked at her again. She felt the heat rise as she took stock of the ramifications of her actions. The emotions pushed through her body like thugs in a crowded bar.

"Huw, I know things have not turned out as I hoped. There was no way I could have anticipated this chaos. But

I really think I need to come clean. To atone for this, somehow. All of us must learn from this incident."

Huw slapped his forehead and sighed in exasperation.

"Maja. Everything we do next needs to protect Gaia Enterprises. We can't let this incident destroy everything we've built. Our world-design philosophy and practice are still sound. Right now, we need to help get Terra Blanca back under control and salvage what we can."

Maja was silent as the two paths lay before her in her mind's eye. She could either own up to her part in the unfolding events or slide along with the current and see if she might steer the boat to calmer waters.

Eventually she nodded. She breathed deeply, letting the shame ebb.

"All right," she said. "The premier said he'd send military support. I'll request early access once they get control back. That way I can assess what is going on and try to contain Luke."

"Let's hope it's not too late." Huw said.

CHAPTER THIRTY-SIX

REGAN WALKED INTO the council Nest with a swagger. He knew it was cocky, but hell! He was riding high on adrenaline, and all charged up. His squad stood around the room, none sitting, blood smeared on some, others wild-eyed, all just as jacked as he was. The energy crackled.

"Justice Squad!" He raised a palm along with his voice. They fell quiet. "Report. Sector 1?"

"Secure," answered a gruff, young man with a bloody tree branch in his hand.

"Citizen accommodation?"

"All locked down." Another young face. *A little pale, that one*, thought Regan. *I'll have to watch him. A little out of his depth.* Regan gave him an encouraging smile.

"The docks?"

"I've left Tony and Brenda down there. No one coming or going," Marty said. Regan eyed his second-in-command. Now here was a reliable asset. He had been right to pick him first. "And the comms? Did Delaware get it done?"

"Yes, sir!" The short, rotund man appeared at the door, and he nudged others out of the way. They made room for him begrudgingly. His belly pulled his shirt into gapes around the buttons.

"Good work, Delaware." Regan favoured him with a beaming smile. Delaware reddened and pushed his thick-rimmed glasses back on his nose. Delaware had been reluctant to participate until Regan offered him the role as head of Innovation Centre once they had things under control. The man had trembled with excitement.

"I heard you caught the governor too, Delaware. Is that right?"

"Yes, sir, I did. She came into the comms tower and I got her with a footstool." He cringed a little at that admission. "I didn't mean to hurt her. I didn't know it was her, actually. I heard the commotion outside and grabbed the footstool for protection. Then she came in and I just swung without thinking."

"It's all right, Delaware. Strange things happen in the heat of the moment. You were only defending yourself." Regan clapped him on the back. "Now, fellas, we need to set the stage here. We are going to have a trial of the council, so look sharp. I'm going to check in on the governor and when she comes to, we'll get this show on the road."

He started up the stairs and then turned back.

"Gentlemen, today we get justice! Today we set Terra Blanca right again!"

Regan pumped a fist. His squad, flushed with victory and anticipation, cheered loudly.

As he bounded up the stairs, Regan had a satisfying sense of destiny.

CHAPTER THIRTY-SEVEN

RYLIE OPENED HER eyes and found herself face-down on the grey carpet of a council meeting room. It was springy and still smelled new. The acrylic fibres pressed into her face as she became aware of drool trickling down her face. She went to move to a sitting position and groaned as her head thrummed in pain. She touched the back of her head gingerly as she sat up. Blood crusted hair against her scalp.

"Governor! Good to see you back among the living." Regan Delarge sat with his ankles crossed and his hands behind his head as if he'd been contemplating the bigger questions in life with all the time in the world.

"Regan." Rylie struggled to her feet.

"Allow me, Governor." Regan jumped up, grabbed her elbow and steered her to a chair.

"What's going on, Regan?"

"Careful, Rylie. You've had quite a nasty bump. George Delaware took a fair crack at you. You surprised him in the comms tower. Man doesn't know his own strength! He's much undervalued, that one."

Rylie felt a wave of nausea curl through her guts.

Regan must have sensed her discomfort because he filled a glass of water from the sideboard and placed it in front of her. That's when she realised Vincent was plugged in, charging in the corner.

"Glad we found you, though," Regan said. "Can't have a trial without the main star."

"What trial?"

"Your trial. For abuse of power. You and your collaborators on the council, of course."

"What poppycock, Regan. There's been no abuse of power."

"Is that so? And what about all your fancy special meals?"

"You can't call a couple of celebration meals 'abuse of power'."

"Oh, no? What about waiving entry requirements? For your daughter's boyfriend?"

Rylie's face became a little paler.

"How did you—?"

"I read the assessment papers. Thanks for not denying it."

"I did that for my daughter."

"I know exactly why you did it. It's called bending the rules for personal gain."

"You don't understand."

"Don't I? I've got a son on the mainland I promised to bring here. Where he could be safe. But now he's doomed to stay stuck in a squalid little squat while your daughter carries on with her lover."

"I'm sorry your family got pushed back, Regan."

"Are you? It doesn't seem like it. I guess you've been too busy selling out Terra Blanca with those ridiculous deals."

"Come on, Regan. They were the best deals I could get. No one else was going to get us food supply."

"Except for maybe Eve's merry band of smugglers. Looks like she's got some good suppliers herself. Maybe you should have asked her for contacts. Did you know she was selling Dopplebot tech for roasts and cheese?"

Rylie looked horrified. "What? That can't be true. She wouldn't…"

Would she? thought Rylie. How well did she really know her daughter? A growing sense of despair threatened to swallow her.

"I swear to you, I don't know anything about that."

Regan stared at her. She did not look away.

"What about the conspiracy to exclude? To undermine?"

"What are you talking about?"

"You excluded me. From many key decisions. And you undermined my authority in the Vertical Farm by allowing all those ridiculous 'objector' investigations. Admit it, you've had it in for me." Regan crossed his arms and stared at her expectantly.

Rylie noticed how his T-shirt sleeves cut into his biceps. Couldn't he find a shirt that fit him? Rylie sipped the water and felt it dilute the nausea a little. Her head ached, and she prodded it again. She winced. She suddenly felt very tired.

"Well?"

"Bloody hell, Regan, you've been a right pain in the ass. From day one. You needled me and council constantly. You've been demanding and critical. You've bullied and cajoled. And we made concession after concession for you. But I have never – not ever – had it in for you."

His blue eyes were like crystal rocks. No one should have eyes like that, thought Rylie. They haunted you.

"Ask Vincent. He'll tell you," she said.

Regan looked over at Vincent, whose eyes were closed. It was a feature Imogen had added early. It was too disconcerting to have the Dopplebot's eyes open all the time. Too inhuman.

"All right. Hey, Vincent."

The Dopplebot's eyes opened and fixed on Regan.

"Vincent, has the governor – and council – have they been railroading me?"

"Please clarify what you mean by 'railroading'."

"Have they been trying to undermine me? Attack my authority?"

"They have not been trying to undermine you. They just don't like you," Vincent said.

Regan stared at Vincent. Then he stared at Rylie.

"You don't like me?" he said finally.

Rylie sighed. They might as well get it all on the table. "You're not that likeable, Regan. You come in all guns blazing. You make demands. You're not at all interested in anyone else." She rubbed her forehead, trying to relieve some pain. She could see the colour rising on his neck. Here we go, she thought.

"You might be right," he said. She was surprised by

this response. "I'm a hard man. From the school of hard knocks, you know."

"We've all had our share of tough times. Through the Big Heat. The drought. All of us have a story."

"What's yours?"

Rylie looked into Regan's eyes and their endless pools of blue.

"My husband was killed in a pilot-training exercise. I've had to raise Eve on my own. I watched the small town where I was on council wither and die. But not before I attended twenty-three funerals. For suicide. Twenty-three. You'd think you'd get used to it. But I never did. Each life snuffed out. Given up. And I swore then I would never give up. On anyone." She held his hard, unblinking gaze. Tears brimmed and rolled but still she met his eyes.

After a while, he leaned back in his chair.

"That's rough, Rylie."

"Yeah."

She sipped some more water and they sat quietly.

"I think it hit Eve more than I realised. That much tragedy and despair when you're young. It crushes the soul."

Regan stayed quiet in the soft gaps between them.

"I watched my bright, bubbly daughter crinkle and dry up with grief when her father died. We both kind of withered, right alongside the town. I think she saw Jared as a lifeline for happiness. Something tender to hang onto in a world full of disappointment and jagged edges."

Rylie rubbed her arm and neck, testing for soreness as she moved a little to get the blood flowing. Regan watched her warily.

"I saw the chance to heal that bitterness a little if we

could get Jared and his family here. Maybe I'd get my little girl back again. It was selfish, I guess."

Regan grunted but said nothing.

Rylie felt for the owl necklace at her throat that Maja had given her. It helped her to feel calm again.

"Being responsible for people. Whether it's as a parent or as a leader, it takes a toll," she said.

"You're not wrong there," Regan said. "Being a leader is like signing up to be a punching bag."

"You've given out as much as you've got, Regan."

"'You're not that likeable, either," he said.

"Oh, no?" Rylie found herself not caring about this insult. The fatigue weighed so heavily.

"No. You're too – too—"

Rylie was about to say "weak" and finish his sentence for him.

"Nice."

She raised an eyebrow at that.

"You have to let everyone have their say," Regan explained. "You consider everyone's point of view. Even when the answer is obvious. It's annoying! Tell her, Vincent! What is Rylie Addison like as governor?"

"Rylie Addison is a pedantic priss," the Dopplebot offered.

"Nice. Thanks for that, Vincent. I'm just following process, Regan. Those are the principles of collective decision-making."

"Sometimes the process is a pain in the ass."

She laughed. "Agreed."

They were quiet for a while. Then Rylie asked, "So, what's *your* story, Regan?"

Regan studied his boots. They were well-worn and scuffed.

"My story…" He snuck a look at Rylie who waited, eyebrows raised.

"Not much to tell, really. I worked hard. Before the Big Heat, I ran a farm supply business. But it dried up when the farms dried up. Had to sell everything. Then they took the house. Ended up in Montreal with the other refugees. I did some salvage work there for a while. Then I got lucky with the Terra Blanca lottery."

"Family?"

Regan grew very still.

"Not anymore. As you know. Paloma left me when it got tough." Regan scratched the back of his head. "Some people can't abide a failure."

"You're not a failure, Regan." Rylie's voice was quiet.

"Ah well. For some, I am."

Silence ran like a river between them.

"Terra Blanca's a chance to prove I could do things right. Provide a home again. Be a father to my little boy." He choked back the lump rising in his throat.

"I'm sorry," Rylie said.

"For what?"

"I wish I'd tried harder. Got to know you better. We could have worked things out."

"We can still work things out, Governor. Just got to follow the process."

"What process? Looks like process is out the window."

"Ye of little faith. We are certainly following process. The boys are setting up the Nest for the trial."

"You can't be serious?"

"I am deadly serious. I've raised the issues, and we will have them resolved. According to council process."

"And how does seizing control of council, bludgeoning people, and locking them up fit into council process?" Rylie asked.

"Council process has become corrupted, we need to put it right again."

"This is crazy, Regan. You know that, right?"

Rylie thought she saw a flicker of doubt. Then his eyes hardened once more.

There was a knock on the door.

"We're ready for you, Boss."

"Thanks, Marty. We're on our way."

Regan stood and opened the door.

"After you, Governor. And you too, Vincent."

The Dopplebot did not budge.

"Would you mind?" Regan asked Rylie.

"Vincent, come with us," she said.

"Thanks, Governor. He's a handy guy to have around. Not afraid of the truth. Apart from that, the process will reveal all."

CHAPTER THIRTY-EIGHT

"OH MY GOD!" cried Rylie as they entered the Nest.

Regan stopped in his tracks.

What the hell? Regan thought.

The heat was suffocating. The noise in the building crashed with galling acoustics.

And down, at the centre of the Nest, was a spectacle it took his brain a moment to process.

His boys had taken a few of the benches from the front row of the stadium and placed them on the big oak table, standing each one on its end.

There were five benches placed this way, lined up. Each one had a short noose strung to the top around the bench legs. Two additional benches were along the length of the upended benches. There were four faces framed by the nooses, and four sets of feet shuffling uneasily on the rickety narrow bench. The fifth noose was empty, waiting.

Luke, Kate, Imogen and Eve looked up in unison at

the sound of Rylie's voice. Mouths gagged, hands bound. Eyes wide with pure and naked fear.

Rylie jumped forward to fly down the stairs, but Regan's big hand clamped on her shoulder.

"No sudden moves, Governor," he said. His mind raced. He had to slow things down. Act calm. In control.

The gallows thing hadn't been part of his briefing. But he could make it work. A bit theatrical, but okay.

He forced himself to saunter down the stairs, gripping Rylie's shoulder, with Vincent trailing.

"Well, gentlemen, thanks for setting the stage." Regan nodded to his minions. "It's a little unnecessary, but I think you've made your point. Untie these people and we can get on with the trial."

Rylie seemed to relax slightly under his grip once she realised he wasn't going to actually hang them. He wasn't a barbarian.

He turned to say something to Vincent.

Then everything went to shit.

CHAPTER THIRTY-NINE

MARTY, REGAN'S CHIEF thug, was rough with him.

"Hey! No need for manhandling," said Luke.

Marty ignored the comment, spun him, grabbed his arms, and pulled them behind his back. Then he tightened a plastic tie around his wrists.

Luke winced. "It's a little tight, Marty."

"Let's go, Finnegan. It's time to face the music."

"Is it now?" Luke said as he turned back to Marty. He searched the man's face, seeing strain pull at the corners of his eyes. A sallowness to the skin. The salty tang of dried sweat with that particular pungency that comes only from deep fear. There were still specks of blood across his shirt.

Marty pulled the fabric of his shirt to see what Luke was looking at. He licked his thumb and tried to rub it out. Tried again. Gave up.

That's interesting, thought Luke.

"Let's go," Marty said.

Marty led him through one of the Nest's internal doors. There was a clamour of activity down on the stage. Some of Regan's men were upending benches onto the council's beautiful oak table.

Those bastards better not scratch it, he thought. All the hours he spent carving the finish into it. It had taken him ages to get the owls just right. It was Maja's personal symbol, and he hadn't wanted to disappoint her.

Marty shoved him down the steps and that's when he caught sight of the other three, bound as he was, sitting a couple of rows up from the stage. Kate was pale and her face twisted in pain. Her shoulders didn't have much flexibility as Luke knew from her sessions in the Wellness Centre. She was leaning forward, trying to get some relief. Her flesh folded over her trousers and the compression effect only made her pant.

Next to her was Imogen, writhing with fury, red-faced and full of vitriol.

"You scum-sucking hordes of horse dung! You have no right to treat us this way! Release us immediately, you limp-dick cowards!" Imogen worked at her restraints to no avail. "Don't worry, Eve, these pathetic excuses for men don't have the courage to do us any real harm."

Eve was still at the end of the bench. Her big brown eyes took in the entire scene. Luke had a sense that she was filing it all away for a story later.

Then he saw a big trembling tear roll down her cheek. His heart broke.

"Come on, guys, at least release the kid for crying out loud. This is crazy." Luke tried to catch someone's eye. They ignored him.

They had the benches upright in a neat row on the oak table now. Then he saw what they were building.

"Gallows? Are you nuts? What is this – the Dark Ages? For Chrissake! You have got to be kidding." Luke turned to Marty, who was still shoving him along towards the others.

"Marty. Do something. You're a reasonable guy. This is going a little too far, don't you think?"

Marty's mouth became a harsh line.

"Got orders," he said.

"Orders. From who? Regan? Even Delarge wouldn't be such an idiot. Come on, now."

Marty had the good sense to blush. But he thrust Luke down on the bench next to Imogen.

"Fuck you, Marty, and the horse you rode in on!" Imogen spat at him.

"Can someone get me some fabric or something? Tea towels? Time these people shut the hell up."

"Way ahead of you, Marty." A young kid, about Eve's age, came over with a fistful of what looked like torn sheets. In his other hand was a large piece of driftwood. "Here's something I prepared earlier," he said with a grin.

"Thanks, Johnny. Can you stand guard over these fuckers while I gag them? Anyone try anything then that's what your stick is for, ok?"

"Got it."

As Marty wadded the material into a fist-sized bundle, Imogen upped her verbal assault.

"You're not going to get away with this, Marty, you pathetic excuse for a man! Such a big tough guy you have to gag us! Can't take the truth, eh? You make me sick, you loathsome cocksucker."

Marty's lips tightened and he went over to Imogen.

"You're first, Princess. Time to teach you some manners."

Imogen spat in his face and tried to kick him in the balls. He stepped easily aside and then slapped her face. He grabbed her hair and yanked her head back so her mouth fell open. He shoved the gag in but not before she managed to bite his finger.

"Fuck!" Marty said and struck her again and shoved the gag back further in her throat. Imogen started to dry heave.

"She's choking!" Luke cried.

Marty watched Imogen's face go purple as she retched and tried to shake the gag out. The heaving stopped, and she breathed nosily through her nose. Tears streamed down her face and a tiny clear balloon of snot formed in one nostril. Marty tied the gag in place.

"Marty, really this has gone too far," Luke tried again. "This isn't like you. I know you. You're a decent guy – show some decency here."

"You know what's gone too far, Finnegan?" Marty came back to Luke and peered into his face. "You. The objectors. The council. All of it. We were just trying to get the job done. Provide food for all of us. All of you. We worked our butts off! And what thanks do we get? Constant criticism. Mocking, by the governor's own daughter, for Chrissake! And then all along you and the rest are gorging on meals we've only been dreaming about. All on Terra Blanca's account. And fudging the residency applications. Giving away the Dopplebots. How can you say you've got Terra Blanca's interests at heart when you're selling us out? Well, it's all over, Red Rover, Finnegan. Time to pay the ferryman."

Wrong expression, a part of Luke's brain murmured. But then Marty grabbed his hair and shoved a wad of material in his mouth and tied it in place. Luke's eyes bulged as he tried to keep from choking.

Kate was sobbing now. She provided no resistance and simply opened her mouth for Marty. Then he walked over to Eve.

"Let me do her."

It was Shane.

"What's the matter, Evie girl? Lost for words now? So easy to be a keyboard warrior, isn't it? Well, I tell you what, girlie, words are weapons. They hurt. It turns out they really do break bones. Just like sticks and stones. Words have consequences. It's time you learned that there are real people at the other end of your nice little stories."

Eve just stared at him with her big, soft brown eyes and the tears ran quietly, unfettered.

"Open wide."

And she did. Luke tried to scream through his gag.

"Now get up there," Marty commanded. He pointed at the oak table. One of the goons was holding a chair as a makeshift step ladder.

Imogen growled at him through her gag. Luke shook his head.

"Either you get up there now or I beat the shit out of Eve until you do." Marty grabbed the driftwood from Johnny and held it over Eve, who tried to hide behind Kate.

Imogen and Luke shouted through their gags. Marty flourished the weapon again.

Imogen stood first. She locked eyes with Marty. With

as much dignity as she could muster, she walked over to the table and stepped up to the gallows.

Luke stood next. He ignored Marty and tried to look encouragingly at Kate and Eve.

It will be all right. We'll be ok. We'll be fine. He willed his thoughts to transmit to the others.

Luke didn't recognise Regan's crew member who guided him to his spot on the bench. Someone grabbed him by the elbow and told him to step up. There were just hands. The rough texture of a rope scratching at his neck. The gag making his mouth water, so he had to swallow awkwardly. Painfully.

Luke's head cleared of thought. Everything seemed to slow and become brilliant and detailed.

There was Rylie's voice. He turned to see her lurch forward. Saw Regan hold her back. Saw a bird fly in through the open door as they came in. A sparrow, most likely. They were always flying in to escape the heat. Someone would have to let it out before it got panicky. Luke noticed the voice in his head was quiet and calm. His voice but not his voice.

Though Regan was at the top of the stairs, Luke saw clearly in his eyes what he hadn't seen before: fear.

This isn't what he wanted, said Luke's quiet voice. *He's in over his head.*

Luke watched Rylie and Regan descend the stairs. They were moving carefully. Vincent the Dopplebot was managing the stairs in his awkward gait, nearly tipping over. Somewhere in a corner of Luke's brain he wondered if Vincent would crush Regan if he did fall over.

The three of them arrived at the stage. Luke saw the terror in Rylie's face as she stared up at her daughter with a noose around her neck. *That must be devastating for a mother,* said Luke's quiet voice.

Luke saw Regan bluster and make light of the situation. Luke heard him tell the goons to release them. Luke saw Regan turn to say something to Vincent.

Then the doors swung open all at once and there were figures in military fatigues and guns and yelling and bodies moving down the stairs in a blur of legs and arms.

They're wet. Why are they wet? asked Luke's quiet voice.

"Freeze! Drop your weapons! Don't move! Sit down!"

The doors were still open. Luke heard the cooling system grind up its effort to account for the influx of sudden heat. He saw the flitter of wings. *Oh good, the sparrow got out,* said Luke's quiet voice.

"Sit down! I said sit down, you big dumb oaf." One of the wet military people was yelling at Vincent.

He's a Dopplebot, said Luke's quiet voice. *Rylie needs to ask him.*

But Luke saw that Rylie only had eyes for her daughter and her face was a mess of pain.

Then Luke saw the military person shove Vincent hard in the chest. He saw the Dopplebot rock back on his heels and topple.

They should really make them more stable, said Luke's quiet voice.

Luke saw the Dopplebot smash against the control button for the stage. He felt the jolt as the table started to lower on its platform.

Kate never did get around to fixing that, said Luke's quiet voice.

Luke felt the panic in four pairs of legs and the scrabble

of four pairs of feet as they tried to regain balance on the wobbly bench. He felt the bench tip away. He felt his feet swing freely. He heard the snapping crunch of bone.

And then… nothing.

CHAPTER FORTY

Three months later

MAJA LOOKED UP as Huw bustled into the meeting room at Gaia Headquarters. She'd been reviewing the footage again.

When the drones had failed to reveal anything, they sent a chopper to get human eyes on the scene. From there they'd worked out the best approach was to send the military with an amphibious assault to avoid the gangs at the docks and along the island shore accommodation.

Maja played the footage again, on slow, for the umpteenth time.

It all happened so fast. The military bursting in, the Dopplebot falling over, the table jolting. Rylie scrambling to grab her daughter's legs, to keep her from dangling.

Too late. They were all too late.

And now there were four dead.

The Terra Blancan leadership wiped out. Terra Blanca was now under Quebec government administration. Rylie and Regan and numerous others detained and under investigation.

Oh, Luke, Maja said to herself.

She rewound the footage and zoomed in on his face, before the bench fell away. His face seemed calm, still.

That's the face I remember.

Maja felt the tears swell and trace her cheeks, drop to her lap.

My love, I am so sorry.

She zoomed in again to Luke's eyes. Brown like her own. Full of light and warmth. A quiet intelligence. The eyes she fell in love with, all those years ago. When they were still kids – students. She'd admired his passion for people; he'd delighted in her creative habitat sketches. They spent hours talking about system and environmental design for better social dynamics.

But then his drinking had swallowed him whole.

He was a quiet drunk. The alcohol dampening whatever pain he had buried even further below the murky surface. His eyes glazed, awash in a dark tide. She couldn't reach him anymore.

So she left.

Then he got sober. So he told her.

By then it was too late. She'd felt herself being dragged into his drowning and couldn't bear it.

She'd followed his career, as one does with past lovers. She'd wondered if he'd kept sober, or just worked out how to hide it better.

He'd send her messages whenever Gaia Enterprises was in the news. Polite congratulations, with brief updates of his own.

Then he reached out when the Terra Blanca lottery was announced.

He was the perfect ally. He understood the social design principles and empathised with what she was hoping to achieve.

She knew he wanted to prove himself to her. Did she take advantage of that?

Maja pushed herself away from the display and went to the window overlooking the training headquarters' central green square. It was quiet. Just the sound of crickets and the chirp of birds in the tree canopy.

The door opened. She knew it was Huw from the bustle.

He joined her at the window.

"So," he said. "What do we know?"

Maja kept staring out the window.

"Still no news. The investigation is ongoing. Regan continues to allege wrongdoing by the council as rationale for the insurrection but denies intent to harm. He claims the hanging was accidental – the result of overzealous, boisterous protesters. No one really wanted to hurt them."

"I see. And Rylie?"

"She denies Regan's accusations. Amazingly, she wants to follow through with Terra Blanca criminal process. She wants to offer Regan and his cronies the option for atonement and redemption."

"Even with her daughter's death. Remarkable. Will the government allow that?"

Maja turned to look at Huw, her face grim. "No. They will not."

Maja returned to the meeting table and turned off the

holo replay. "The government has refused to return Terra Blanca to independent governance under the current circumstances. We are back to conventional rule."

"I see," Huw said, and joined her at the table. "I'm sorry, Maja. I know this was more than just a building project for you."

They sat quietly for a few minutes.

"And what of Luke? Does anyone know?"

"It appears not. There is no evidence in any of the council recordings of his intent to challenge process. If anything, his part as an objector places him firmly against the insurrectionists, not as an instigator."

"What was that about? Do you know?"

"No. As you know, we had no communications. I can only guess that Luke felt the damage being done by Regan went beyond just challenging the system. Like me, Luke never wanted to destroy the thing we built. Just test its weaknesses."

"It looks like we found some pretty big weaknesses."

"Yes. But not where we thought."

"How do you mean?"

"The system could still work, I think. It just didn't account for a few variables."

"Such as?"

"The storm. The survivors. The people." She hesitated, then went on, "It's the people."

"Who are you blaming, Maja?"

"Not blaming, Huw. The system was up to it. The people were not. A system is only as strong as the people who manage it. The system would have been fine for people who had a little more maturity. A little more self-awareness.

We didn't screen well enough for that. We relied heavily on skills in the profiles, and not enough on interpersonal resilience and sensitivity."

"But we did extensive interviews."

"Anyone can look good on paper. A good actor can charm at interview. It wasn't enough. We need to see people under pressure. Real pressure."

Maja rubbed her neck. Everything ached since the Terra Blanca incident.

"The biggest mistake I made was with Rylie. I thought she'd be up to it, given what she had been through on the mainland. But it seems little choices rolled into big mistakes."

"So, the problem was in recruitment?"

"Partly. They did not have the leadership maturity to handle a community like that – isolated and self-contained."

"But shouldn't we have built a system that could account for all levels of maturity?"

"Probably. Yes." Maja shuffled the papers on the desk and picked up a pencil. "I was hoping the system would build the maturity for them. That they would grow into it."

"But they didn't."

"No, they didn't." Maja bent over her sketches. "People need a little more support and guidance. We can't just dump people in a system and hope for the best."

Maja guided the pencil softly over the paper.

"Huw, four people are dead because of our failed experiment. One of them a child who hadn't even started her life yet."

"We're not to blame for all of that."

"Aren't we?"

Her smooth brown face turned to his. Ghosts haunted her eyes. Huw saw the grief and distress wringing her soul.

"I'm going to take a break for a while, Huw. I'll be on-hand for the investigation, of course. I'll be fully contactable."

"Where will you go?"

"I'll stay at Headquarters until the inquiry is over. Then I thought I might go to the desert."

"Why there?"

"There's something about wide open spaces and ancient lands that have a way of healing hearts."

Huw watched her draw for a while.

"What is that?" he asked.

"It's a new emblem. I've added a heart around the owl."

"Nice."

Maja put her pencil down and looked earnestly at Huw.

"Huw, I will do better. I promise."

He covered her long slender fingers with his own warm, thick ones.

"We," he said. "*We* will do better."

He smiled at her. She smiled back.

AUTHOR'S NOTE

Thank you so much for reading *Terra Blanca*, the prequel to the Gaia series. It's a privilege to be in front of your eyeballs, or if you're listening to the audiobook, in your ears.

If you enjoyed the book, I would be deeply grateful for a review on *Amazon*, *Goodreads*, or *BookBub*. It would be awesome if you could follow me there, too. As I am an Indie author, reviews help get the word out and help other readers enjoy the growing Gaia universe. With so much competition, and with limited resources compared to the major publishing houses and the big distribution platforms, your few sentences about the book really do make a huge difference.

Please join our monthly-ish e-journal *BOOKISH*. I give updates on works in progress, special bonus extras like cover reveals and character interviews, along with book reviews, for leadership and fiction. Join us here: *https://www.zoerouth.com/bookish*

I'd love to hear from you! Tell me what you loved, or didn't, about the book. Tell me if you find typos or weird phrasings. Even with professional editing and proofreading, and a small army of friends to check it, those little rascals can still sneak through. Email me: zoe@zoerouth.com.

THE AI ASSISTED
ARTISAN AUTHOR: A4

Joanna Penn, one of my writing mentors, coined this term. In her deep exposes of how to use A.I. ethically as an author, she explains how we can benefit by having A.I. as a co-pilot for unique, creative output. I subscribe to this view.

With all the hoopla going around about artificial intelligence, I thought I would share how I use A.I. apps in my creative process. I work with Scrivener as a writing platform and use ProWritingAid to help review grammar, syntax, writing ticks and glitches. I use *thesaurus.com* for word variation and Chat GPT-4 for research and ideas. I also used it to help generate the book blurb. Like most writers, I find book blurbs arduous and Chat GPT4 made that a little easier. I used Midjourney to generate the background image cover, and humans at Damonza did the final production. Humans also helped with the fine-tuning: big thanks to Darren Nash for forthright critique and edits, and Abigail Nathan for proofreading. With new apps coming out every day, no doubt my process will change again for the next novel.

And on the subject of other novels, please read on to discover more of the Gaia world. *The Olympus Project* picks up a few years after *Terra Blanca*. Maja Garcia is embarking on a bold new endeavour that could chart a new direction for humanity.

THE
OLYMPUS
PROJECT

GAIA BOOK 1

ZOË ROUTH

CHAPTER ONE

*Humans evolve in their environment. If we can create
environments that expand the human spirit, we have a
chance of calling forward mankind's better nature.*

THE WORLD DESIGNERS' MANIFESTO

Sydney: Xanthe

THE SPACESUIT PRESSED down on her like a lead blanket.
The chair rattled and shook her violently. Xanthe felt the
skin of her face grow taut and strained. Suddenly there was
weightlessness. Relief. And the view of the world below: a
soft, blue, mottled curve against the black forever of space.
Awe swelled within her as it did every time she snuck in to
the VR simulation hub for a joy ride.

All too soon, they re-entered the Earth's orbit, landed,
and the lights burned bright, assaulting her senses. Back
now in the VR room with its bland walls and disappointing
reality. Xanthe trudged into the change room, along with

the other punters, and stripped off her well-worn hired sensor suit. She slipped out to the stinking hot streets of Sydney.

Poor Sydney. A pale version of its former glorious self. The city had survived the long years of COVID-19, the first pandemic. But then subsequent viruses had sent city dwellers scurrying for the country. Towering office blocks stood empty, like soulless sentinels. The ground-floor windows, at first bright with hopeful "For Lease" signs, were now boarded up and smattered with graffiti. The "For Sale" signs came next and fell, like autumn leaves, trodden underfoot. The tsunami washed out the rest, wrecking the beautiful harbour with a devastating backwash. It was only when the drought and the rising inland heat sent people back to the coast that Sydney had experienced its latest renaissance. Old commercial properties were repurposed for inner-city living. New density requirements crammed people into renovated eco-buildings, brimming inside with vertical greenery, coated on the outside with plants to keep the structures cool. These often formed a hydroponic sleeve, feeding the building's inhabitants with a vertical farm.

Xanthe stopped on a corner and looked up. It was one of her prized projects. As chief designer, she had turned this old corporate tower into a family oasis. The entrance was resplendent with trees and tropical flowers. The exterior heaved with plant life and a few remaining birds, grateful for a cool haven. Her smartest innovations were the network of clear-plastic tunnel slides that allowed people to navigate quickly between floors, and habitat stations with ladders on the outside. She had managed to create a community where all food, entertainment and social inter-actions were self-contained. No one needed to brave the heat of the day ever again. She called it "The Pantheon" She smiled at the arrogance. Hell, she'd earned the right.

Xanthe took another moment and squinted up at The Pantheon, then pulled the sunshade over her brow. It was barely dawn, but the heat was baking already. It was late to be out, and Simon would be waiting.

Simon could always tell when she'd been to the VR Hub. Was it the longing she tried desperately to hide? The telltale stench of sweat from the overused VR suit still clinging to her? The disdain would crawl across his face. "Why do you bother? Falling into the crass, commercial claws of the Big Tech oligarchies. Such a betrayal…" and the lecture would continue, always the same, always bitter. He was an Earth Advocate, as she had been. Still was. Mostly.

Simon was committed to the salvation of the planet. He believed that technology should be deployed to rectify the climate disasters that ravaged Earth, not for some bil-lionaire's folly to colonise other planets. He did appreciate that life on Earth was ultimately doomed, since it would eventually boil dry as it approached the expanding sun. But that was still billions of years away. Life was happening *now*. Whichever philosophical or spiritual lens you put on it, Earth was humanity's home, and we should embrace our fate alongside it. Why poison other planets with our ineptitude? Better to get the management of this one right.

Xanthe heard his words echo from their last argument. She agreed with him on many points. Yes, Earth was sacred. Yes, it was beautiful and worth saving. But, she tried to add in spite of his eye-rolling, consciousness was valuable too, and we have a moral obligation to help it survive our planet's eventual doom. That usually sparked a diatribe about the responsibilities of the wealthy and the outrageous waste of money on space tourism. She often backed down at this point. It was hard to argue about the money side of things.

Xanthe wasn't quite ready for another confrontation. She took the long way home and headed towards the harbour. It drew her there. The sea's siren songs plucked her heart strings, mournful. There on the harbour, the dawn licked the sky with a harsh red tongue. Xanthe felt the rush of the tsunami once again. The dreadful roar and the incomprehensible power of the water that picked her up and threw her forward in a turbulence that choked all other sound. It was a moment, only a moment. The relief of breath. Then the awful realisation of loss. So much horrible loss.

As a paramedic, she had found the despair overwhelming. So many people she tried to save and couldn't. So many people lost. As the grief subsided, Xanthe found new purpose in the wake of the tsunami. She abandoned her job and dived into cleaning up the city. She worked first with the salvage crews, then trained with Gaia Enterprises to design new communities. She believed in resurrection, in renewal. The Phoenix, Lazarus, and all those old tales. They would make something glorious of this wrecked, debris-strewn city. They would find beauty even as the world tore her heart in two. They would salvage what they could from the vengeful Earth and create something wonderful, beautiful and worth living for.

"I thought I'd find you here."

Xanthe jumped a little, startled from her reverie, and turned away from the water she had been staring over.

"Maja." Though she was surprised, her voice came out flat. "What are you doing here?"

Xanthe eyed the older woman with her impossibly smooth, brown skin, and noticed the trace of a few lines at the corner of her eyes, deeper now than when she had last seen her.

"I've come to see you." Maja's face was gentle, filled with love, her dark eyes deep.

You could swim in those eyes, thought Xanthe. *Drown in them.* She shuddered slightly.

"How are you, Xanthe?"

Xanthe considered Maja, then looked out again at the water. A wind stirred the surface. The hot wind rising already.

"I'm fine." They both knew it wasn't true. But true enough.

Maja took Xanthe's arm in hers and steered her along the shore that was one of the first areas they had repaired. People needed a place to go. To think. To breathe.

"Why are you here, Maja?" Xanthe knew Maja did not make house calls for former employees.

"We've got a new project to tender for," Maja said.

Xanthe frowned. Why not use the holocall? Since when did a project tender require in-person visits? Xanthe waited and let the silence draw Maja's words from her.

"It's something new for Gaia Enterprises. Something… audacious."

Xanthe found this surprising. "Audacious? Gaia has always been audacious, Maja. It's why I joined in the first place. Land reclamation communities that span the globe. Floating worlds. Rebuilding flood-ravaged cities. And what could be more audacious than the underwater worlds?"

Xanthe stopped to look Maja full in the face. What was she playing at? Gaia Enterprises had been one of the salvations of climate-change-ravaged Earth. After the droughts, the tsunamis, the rising sea levels, Gaia was helping humanity adapt to the devastation. It was creating new habitats. *Although, not fast enough*, thought Xanthe. Climate refugees were clinging to life, eking out an existence close to the water, living in the shadows during the day to stay out of the heat. Even now she could feel their eyes on her and Maja, from their hiding places in the rubble of ruined buildings, in makeshift shanties. Xanthe and Maja were out too late in the day already. The sun burned the air around them. Xanthe felt the sweat soaking her thin cotton robe. Desert wear. In a city by the sea.

"What new project, Maja?"

Maja held her gaze, then looked away. "We are putting in a bid for the Moon."

Xanthe stared, aghast. "You're kidding!" she cried. "The Moon? Since when did Gaia abandon Earth?" This went against all Gaia principles. As its very name indicated, Gaia was about the Earth, not space.

"I know it sounds like a – a change."

"A change! This is sacrilege! Gaia Enterprises is about restoring human life on planet Earth! For years we've battled the Space Cowboys and their crazy quest to colonise Mars! All that money! All those resources that could be saving lives – here – on Earth," Xanthe fumed. And she heard it too in her own words: *for years we've battled…* We. Even after all these years, she still felt the "we". The pull back to her designer origins.

Maja waited until Xanthe had vented her outrage.

"I thought the same. At first." Again, Maja hooked her arm through Xanthe's, and guided her towards some shade at the corner of an old building. "But this is an opportunity to promote Gaia's work and vision here on Earth. A Moon project will show how beautiful Earth is. How it is worth preserving. Worth saving. There is no better view of the planet than from space. As you well know."

Xanthe froze. How did Maja know about her VR Hub visits? She kept it all a secret, except from Simon. *Simon.* Damn him. He must have told Maja. His own bitterness and frustration. The old wound between them, a heaviness like a scab on their relationship, big and ugly and misshapen, even as it aimed to protect them both from the cancerous pain.

"Why are you telling me this, Maja? I'm not part of Gaia's pool of designers anymore."

"I know. But we're making a special callout. We need skills like yours. You've got the medical background and successful world-design experience. Perfect for the complex designs needed for the Moon – and I personally appreciate your community focus." She paused and glanced at Xanthe. "I know you didn't like the direction Gaia was heading with its commercial decisions, but sometimes leadership means making choices that look bad in the short term, if the long term is served."

"Come on, Maja, I don't buy into the ends justifying the means. It looked like a sellout to me."

"I prefer to think of it as a 'borrow-in'."

"Really? Gaia Enterprises agreed to build a new Disney-land, for crying out loud! Hardly helping climate refugees, as far as I can see."

Maja smiled at that. "There's always room for joy in the

world, Xanthe. Besides, that project allowed us to invest in terraforming technology. Not everything that looks like indulgence has no value.

"In any case, Gaia has gone from strength to strength. The worlds we've built are creating new hope for people around the planet. For its part, the Olympus Project is a little like the Disneyland one, except that the outcome isn't just joyrides. It's also asteroid mining and research. If we win the bid, it will give us another revenue stream that will advance our Earth salvage mission. And we'll take an ongoing management fee once the base is established. That fee will fund multiple projects we've been longing to launch here on Earth."

Xanthe was quiet as she considered Maja's elaborate business plans.

Maja continued. "We're opening up selection for the Olympus Project bid to applicants from other design companies. No more than one applicant per company to try and narrow the pool. We're expecting a huge amount of interest. Gaia has never opened its doors to other designers, and we suspect there will be a few wanting to get a foot in. We're running a selection to put together a design and deliver team. The team will work the prototype as part of the project bid. If the bid is successful, that team will build the project together. On the Moon."

Xanthe gasped. Off-planet world-building! It wasn't just about the design; it was the build, too! But regardless of what Maja said, it was the antithesis of Gaia. Why were they abandoning their principles? If you can't beat 'em, join 'em? Selling the value of Earth, from space? Come on. There was more going on here than some possible future management fee.

The Moon. Against her will, Xanthe's heart pounded with excitement. The VR Hub had been her secret indulgence, a place to escape the pain that dogged her days on Earth. The chance to actually travel off-world, to space, to the Moon. Was she a hypocrite for wanting to experience the beauty of Earth from afar? Maybe it would help her to find some peace again. Or maybe she just wanted to run away. And the Moon was about as far away as she could get. For now. The Mars plan was not quite in reach, in spite of the billions the Space Cowboys had thrown at it – not to mention the twenty-six lives already burned in the pursuit.

"What do you want from me?" Xanthe asked finally.

"I want you to be part of the core design team. We need three lead designers, and then a pilot, mechanic and life-support specialist to make up the team of six. Gaia would like you to be the third designer. With your medical background and proven community-design skills, you'd balance the team nicely."

"Wow. I'm honoured. Shocked, but honoured. I need some time to think about this, Maja."

"Of course. It's a big commitment."

"Just out of interest, who are the other two?"

"Troy Bruin and Xavier Consus."

"Oh my God! The superstars!"

Maja smiled. She was proud of these Gaia designers and was always delighted by the impression they made.

Xanthe took a deep breath. "Okay, tell me more," she said.

CONTINUE READING

THE OLYMPUS PROJECT

ON AMAZON

Or buy direct from me, the author:

https://www.zoerouth.com/the-olympus-project

ACKNOWLEDGMENTS

Writing is a quiet solitary endeavour, with hysterics in the background. There is plenty of teeth-gnashing, late night plot-mulling, and unhelpful stress-eating.

A.I. can't cure many of those ills. But friends and colleagues can.

Big thanks to my editor, Darren Nash, for his witty and helpful feedback and for saving the manuscript from gaping holes in logic. More thanks to Abigail Nathan who wielded a very good proofreading magnifying glass. The team at Damonza did another outstanding cover design – thanks!

Big hugs and gratitude to Benny Callaghan and Jon Dell'Oro who critiqued the manuscript and offered insightful feedback. I really appreciate your support and enthusiasm.

And a big warm hug and thank you to my Outward Bound friends who asked me excitedly about the next novel and made suggestions for vignettes. I enjoyed building some of those into the story. Thanks for being a safe place to land. And for guaranteed good laughs!

To my wonderful husband, thanks for promoting my work on the golf course and to anyone who will listen.

And thanks to my family, who put up with me, and continue to be my best fans and supporters.

And to Marcelo Silveira, an Outward Bound friend who died while I was writing this book, thank you for being an inspiration for living well. Life is a grand adventure after all and we return to stardust soon enough. So, carpe diem!

ABOUT THE AUTHOR

Zoë Routh is a leadership futurist, podcaster, and multiple award-winning author. She works with leaders and teams to explore what's coming and what it means for leadership of the future.

She has worked with individuals and teams internationally and in Australia since 1987. From wild Canadian rivers to the Australian Outback with Outward Bound, and the Boardroom jungles, Zoë is an adventurist! She facilitates strategy and culture for the future with audacious teams.

Zoë is the producer of the Zoë Routh Leadership Podcast, dedicated to asking "What if…?" and sharing big ideas on the Future of Leadership.

Zoë is an outdoor adventurist and enjoys telemark skiing, has run six marathons, is a one-time belly-dancer, has survived cancer, and loves hiking in the high country. Zoë lives in Canberra, Australia with her gorgeous Aussie husband, where you'll find her running, baking, and reading.

Follow Zoë on Amazon and Goodreads and Book Bub

https://www.zoerouth.com

https://www.facebook.com/zoe.routh

https://twitter.com/zoerouth

https://au.linkedin.com/in/zoerouth

https://www.instagram.com/zoerouth

https://www.youtube.com/c/ZoeRouthInnerCompass/

zoe@zoerouth.com

www.ingramcontent.com/pod-product-compliance
Lightning Source LLC
Chambersburg PA
CBHW020006140726
47904CB00018B/1981